MW00426083

The Leadership Road:
Positive Actions
That Drive Results

Robert C. Preziosi

Llumina Press

ISBN: 978-1-59526-772-6

Printed in the United States of America by Llumina Press

Library of Congress Control Number: 2007901650

This book is dedicated to
all of my past, present, and future students.

Acknowledgements

Many of my colleagues urged me to write this book and kept me focused on it. Many thanks to Preston Jones, Barry Barnes, Doreen Gooden, Bill Harrington, Bill Johnson, Bahaudin Mujtaba, and Rita Smith.

The book became a reality thanks to Arlette Ballew, a world-class development editor. Her ongoing editing and other feedback helped me turn my ideas and writing into a book worthy of publication. She made it better every step of the way.

I appreciate the work of Deborah Greenspan, the publisher at Lumina Press. She and her folks did a great job getting this book out.

Barbara Ireland was the key in putting it all together. She word processed with lots of care. She made the revisions I asked for. She kept me and the project very well organized.

My daughters, Lauren Marie and Carly Elizabeth, and Carly's husband, Dan, always helped me keep things in perspective.

Most importantly, though, was the ongoing positive and optimistic point of view provided by my wife, Kitty. She urged me on and made sure that the book would be of high quality. She made suggestions for tweaking things from the beginning to the end. She was inspiring!

Many thanks to the Lord for giving me the talent to complete this project.

Table of Contents

Preface

It has been said that people should be slow to speak and quick to listen. During my experiences as an academic leader, business leader, and volunteer leader, I have tried to do exactly that.

Most of what we know about leadership was written by educators, theoreticians, consultants, and other such people. However, I think that the people who have worked in organizations and have seen leaders be successful or unsuccessful have a great deal of information to offer. So this book is based on what I have heard people say about successful leadership for more than twenty-two years. The people I have worked with always have had a lot to say about what was done well and what was not done well in their organizations. My graduate business students have written thousands of papers about what works and what doesn't, and we talk about this continually in class. My students are unique because they are not traditional students. They all have professional or executive jobs, and some of them run their own companies. So they have very useful information to share about the real world of leadership.

I have a lot of leadership experience myself. Through the years, I've settled on a model that helps me understand and provide a framework for discussions of leadership, for leadership training, and for leadership education. The purpose of this book is to share what I've learned about successful leadership in organizations. I know that the advice offered here is sound, because people who work in business, government, and not-for-profit organizations all have validated the model that this book presents.

The foundation for the model comes from experiences with what is successful, not just in my opinion but from the perspectives of people who work day to day in large and small businesses and other organizations—ones that have small markets as well as those that consider the world their market. I have combined their wisdom and experience in this book, along with what I've seen that makes solid leaders what they are. It is a synopsis of what leaders have to *do*, and what leaders have to *be* in order to be successful as leaders.

Robert C. Preziosi
Davie, Florida
August, 2008

Introduction

My students have written hundreds of thousands of pages about leadership in their organizations. They have been more than casual observers in writing about the things that they think successful leaders do. They also have written about the things that leaders haven't done well.

These students have come from business, government, educational, and not-for-profit organizations. They have been observers of leadership in action and have been directly involved in leading. This has provided an opportunity for analysis that is quite unique.

I have had students from five continents, although probably 90 percent of them have been from North America. Their average age is between twenty-nine and thirty-three, with some of them in their early twenties and some well into their fifties. All of them have had unique vantage points because they have worked as professionals, supervisors, managers, executives, and entrepreneurs.

I have always asked them to write about the successful actions they have seen leaders take, and I have always asked them to be as objective as possible. The only deterrent to their objectivity might be lack of self-awareness in analyzing their own actions.

I have prodded them to find ways to make the leadership better in their organizations. My approach is not to prove the truth of any particular theory about leadership behavior. Rather, I have asked them to take an action research perspective and to identify what they think needs to be done. The action research model is standard: 1) data collection, 2) data feedback, 3) program planning and implementation, and 4) evaluation.

In using this action research model, I have been conducting a kind of field study. Although we normally speak of a field study as an approach to studying one organization, this particular field study cuts across a wide variety of organizations. I do not suggest that this book provides a universal set of truths, but the actions described have worked in a wide variety of organizations.

The Reasons for This Book

I decided to write this book for a few reasons. First, there continues to be a need to converse about leadership so that we can better understand it. The ongoing exchange of information about successful acts of leadership can broaden the understanding and impact that people in leadership positions have. This improves their leadership experiences.

Second, I have worked for some terrific leaders and have been a leader. They knew, and I have learned, that without viewing and analyzing the acts of others, we have no basis for comparison in terms of our own leadership. We learn not only from our own successes and failures but also from the successes and failures of others.

Third, as well as leading and teaching leadership, I have been a student of leadership. While I was in junior high school, other kids always wanted me to be a captain when we picked sides for playground sports. In high school, I had a variety of leadership experiences as president of various organizations and as a captain of a high school sports team. These youthful leadership experiences led me to want to be a leader and to teach leadership. From then on through college and beyond, I paid attention to how people responded to my acts of leadership. It is obvious to me now that I listened a lot and I knew how to pick and use talent. It is also clear that I knew how important both positive and negative reinforcement are and how essential it is to celebrate success.

In high school, I studied leaders in history. In college, I studied the behaviors of leaders. Early on, I was exposed to Hersey and Blanchard's model of Situational Leadership. It has always been a driving force for me when I am teaching others how important it is to be flexible in your leadership activities. Later, I gained tremendous help in understanding successful leadership from the works of people such as Warren Bennis, Max DePree, and Jim Kouzes and Barry Posner. My students have provided me with thousands of hours of positive value as I have read what they had to say about leadership in their organizations. It just seems fitting that this information be shared.

In the spirit of appreciative inquiry and appreciative learning, I have tried not to include any negativity in this book. Appreciative inquiry is an organization development (OD) intervention that requires an internal or external constant to assess what is being done right or properly in an organization and then to find ways to implement those things throughout the organization. Appreciative inquiry also offers the option of going forward in a positive way by imagining a positive future in the things that have to be done or accomplished in order to create that future. This may sound like "best practices" to you and, indeed, best practices are first cousins of this methodology.

What Is Leadership?

A book about leadership certainly should provide a definition of what leadership is. In my leading, teaching, and consulting, I have noticed how our understanding of leadership behaviors continues to expand. Recently, I have been talking about the 21st Century's definition of leadership. It is actions committed by a person or group that produce an output or result. Leadership simply helps people to get things done.

I firmly believe that this means that we are all leaders, regardless of our functional titles or positions on an organizational chart. There always will be people with titles such as president, general manager, principal, city manager, and prime minister. These are people who sit at the top of organizational charts. Because of their vantage points and their positions, the actions they take have broad impact. Everyone else has impact, too. It just tends to be more focused, because our domains are smaller than those of the people at the top of the organizational charts.

Leadership Tasks and Values

As I have read student papers and discussed leadership actions in my classes, I have noticed that certain themes continue to surface. These themes are easily separated into two categories: tasks and values. Not every student wrote about or discussed every task or value included in this book. However, there are dominant themes, and I have heard them consistently for twenty-two years from the majority of my students.

This book is more than a report of students' observations. I have included what I call suggestions for action. The suggestions include approaches and behaviors that lead to successful leadership. The following tasks have been identified over the years as having the most positive impact: 1) develop congruence of vision and values, 2) link strategic elements of the organization, 3) use fact-based decision making, 4) create an atmosphere for open communication, 5) manage change, 6) manage conflict, 7) manage performance, 8) coach for results, 9) develop a business-process orientation, 10) reinforce high-performance teaming actions, 11) establish a customer-service management system, and 12) establish a productivity-planning initiative.

There also are twelve values that my students have consistently identified: 1) courage, 2) creativity, 3) diversity, 4) equity, 5) fairness, 6) honesty, 7) humor, 8) integrity, 9) optimism, 10) respect, 11) risk taking, and 12) trust.

I would like to mention three focus groups that were conducted in 2000 by the Hudson Institute of Entrepreneurship and Executive Education. The focus groups included successful leaders, HR executives, and training executives from business and government. The members ranged in age from about thirty-two to about sixty. They came from southeastern Florida—one of the largest urban areas in the United States. What these focus groups produced in the way of curriculum areas for the development of leaders was remarkable. Their efforts led to the development of a Leadership Impact lab. Their content areas had much in common with what my students had been writing about for more than twenty-two years. The content areas that they thought were important are: 1) sustainability, 2) values alignment, 3) leading change, 4) customer focus, 5) risk taking and courage, 6) managing performance, 7) creativity and innovation, 8) high-performance teams, 9) leader as coach, 10) developing others, 11) feedback analysis, 12) avoiding derailment, 13) building interpersonal connections, 14) achieving results, 15) building credibility, and 16) business processes.

The commonality between my students' work and the focus groups' list emphasizes how much agreement there is about what leadership behaviors and characteristics are important. My students, though, have wisely identified many aspects of productivity as the major focus required of leaders.

How This Book Is Organized

Each leadership task is the focus of a separate chapter, while the values are explained in a single chapter. At the end of each chapter, I include a series of questions that the reader should spend time thinking about. All of us need to spend more time reflecting about what we read before we put it into action and before we congratulate ourselves by saying, "We knew that" or "We already do that."

List of Organizations

The following is a partial listing of organizations that my students have belonged to or worked in over the years. The purpose of the list is to enable you to understand the impact that these students and their organizations have had on this book.

Air Jamaica	Alamo Rental Car
American Airlines	American Express
American International Bank	American Lung Association
Amgen	Andrx
Aramark	Arby's
Astra Merck	AT&T
AutoNation	Bahamas Air
Banco Santander	Bank of America
BankAtlantic	Baptist Hospital
Baxter	Beaches Resorts
Bell South	Black and Decker
Blockbuster	Blue Cross/Blue Shield
Blue Mountain	Bluegreen
Broward County Government	Broward Public Schools
Budget Rent A Car	Burdines-Macys
Burger King	Cable and Wireless

Carnival Cruise Lines

Charles Schwab

CIGNA

Citibank

City of Miami Beach

Coach Leather Goods

Columbia/HCA

Del Monte

Delta Air Lines

Dole

Enterprise Rent-A-Car

Federal Bureau of Investigation

Federated Department Stores

First Union

Florida Power & Light

Florida Marlins

Ford Motor Credit

General Electric

GL Homes

GMAC

Hallmark

Harris Corporation

Hertz

IBM

Ivax Technologies

Centex Construction

Chevron

Cingular

Citrix

Cleveland Clinic

Coca-Cola

Dade County Public Schools

Davie, Florida

DHL

Dun & Bradstreet

Ericsson

Federal Express

First Data

Florida Power Corporation

Florida International University

Florida Panthers

Franklin Templeton

General Motors

Glaxo Wellcome

Grainger International

Harcourt

HealthSouth

Home Shopping Network

Intel

Internal Revenue Service

Jim Walter Corporation	JM Family Enterprises
Johnson Controls	Johnson & Johnson
Kaiser Aluminum	Keiser College
Kos Pharmaceuticals	Leadership Broward
Lennar	Eli Lilly
Marriott	Martin Marietta
Miami Dade College	Merrill Lynch
Miami-Dade County	Miami Dolphins
Miami Heat	Miami Herald
Motorola NCCI	Norwegian Cruise Line
Nestlé	North Broward Hospital District
Novartis	Nova Southeastern University
Ocean Grill	Office Depot
Orlando Regional Medical Center	Pembroke Pines
Pepsi	Port Everglades
Pompano Beach	Post, Buckley, Schuh & Jernigan
Prudential	Publix Super Markets
Quaker Oats	Racal Datacom
Raymond James Financial Services	Royal Caribbean Cruise Lines
Republic Services	Ritz Carlton
Rockwell	Rubbermaid
Schering Plough	Service America
Sheraton	Siemens
SmithKline	South Broward Hospital District
SouthTrust (Wachovia)	Sports Authority

Sprint	SSA Global
Sun Sentinel	SunTrust
SuperClubs	Sysco
Tenet Healthcare Corporation	Tropicana
Transportation Security Admin.	Tyco International
University of Phoenix	University of Florida
University of Miami	United Parcel Service
U.S. Air Force	U.S. Army
U.S. Marines	U.S. Navy
Valencia Community College	Verizon
Visa	Wachovia Bank
Walgreens	Walt Disney World
Westin Hotels and Resorts	Westinghouse

Chapter 1

Develop Vision and Values Congruence

I was about fourteen years old when I found myself in a fistfight. It wasn't my idea but, at the time, it seemed like an appropriate response although it was with one of my best friends. In any case it taught me something about values.

The fight probably lasted about forty-five seconds. I was thinner then, so my dazzling foot speed didn't allow my friend to land a punch. I took a couple of swings. One of them actually hit something, because I noticed after the fight that my friend's nose was bleeding. It wasn't very bad but, of course, I was sorry that it had happened.

Because the fight happened at the end of our block, my mother found out about it. I was sent to my room and was told to think about why the fight had happened and why it shouldn't happen again. I guess I didn't have any homework that afternoon because I actually thought about it.

Although I had been very competitive in sports, drama, and public speaking, I was typically collaborative in working with other kids. I valued harmony. I realized that my friend always seemed to be looking for a fight. He and I hadn't had one before that because we were such close friends and he was always busy fighting with other kids. As I

1

thought about what had happened, I realized that not only was my friend disharmonious, he also didn't believe in a superior being or have a sense of spirituality. His approach in dealing with others was not what I called honest. These were some of the differences that I noted as I thought about what had happened that afternoon. It was then that I realized that people liked different things and behaved in different ways. This was my first encounter with something called *values discrepancy*. It seemed very odd to me. I wondered why there wasn't greater agreement.

The Importance of Vision and Values Congruence

The participants in my studies have looked at this from different perspectives. First, they speak in terms of how important vision and values congruence is. It is probably the easiest congruence to obtain. Second, they speak about congruence between an organization's vision and a person's individual vision, which is important to motivation. The final way in which they think about such congruence is between the values that an individual holds and the values that an organization holds.

Many people believe that the idea of vision and values as leadership tools is new. However, you can go back centuries and see examples of how vision and values, when aligned, are strong motivating forces. One example is the early Roman Empire. Every Roman knew what Rome stood for and what behaviors were expected of Roman citizens. Southwest Airlines is a perfect example of how vision and values drive business success, as is Apple Computer's imagination about the future (vision) and new-product launches by committed employees (values). Vision and values have become major forces in successful business and governmental organizations in the 21st Century.

Developing Organizational Vision and Mission Statements

Organizations and individuals have visions of the future that drive their behaviors, whether they realize it or not. An organization may have a vision statement or a mission statement or both. Usually these are written and may appear on the organization's web site, advertising materials, and/or business cards. I've seen vision and mission statements on posters in employee lounges and on employee bulletin boards.

In some organizations, neither has been written down nor expressed in a formal manner. In such organizations, it may be clear that there is a vision or mission that is driving the organization, but the leaders of the organization have inadvertently or purposely chosen not to have the vision or mission on display. In such cases, the employees do not have a sense of what the overall purpose of the organization is (other than to make money). Studies reported by the Drucker Foundation have shown that people need reasons for their work, and the more value they see in their work, the more motivated they are. When the vision and mission are articulated, the work force is more focused. The vision and mission provide goals and a focus for energy that leads to better task performance.

Organizational visions usually are based on the answer to the question, "What do we want to be?" Organizational leaders normally

3

identify the vision and mission during a strategic planning process, but they can be identified in other ways. In one organization, the vision statement may be developed in a shared fashion with groups of employees. In another organization, the vision and mission may be established by the chief operating officer, board chairperson, or a high-level management or policy-making group. Each statement usually is not more than a few sentences, but it should be clear about where the organization wants to focus its efforts.

Identifying Organizational Values

Once an organization's leaders are clear about what its vision is and what its mission is, they must identify categories of thoughts and behaviors they believe will make the vision and mission a reality. The broad categories of what people believe in and then express in their behaviors are often referred to as *values.*

In the early 1970s, when I was involved in the values-clarification movement with Dr. Sidney B. Simon, it was very clear to me that it was easy to know exactly what a value is. A value is defined as a force that a person or an organization is willing to act on over and over again in a consistent way after having considered alternatives and consequences for every possible "behavior." That definition is reinforced in the conversations that my students have with me and with one another.

An organization's values support its vision, so organizations usually espouse values that are consistent with their visions. Popular business magazines and journals publish articles saying how important values congruence is and the effect it can have on business results. There are many examples in the business literature of organizational vision and value statements, and anybody can review them to identify the congruence or lack of it.

However, it is possible for an organization to reflect values that are not consistent with its vision. The incongruence usually leads to destructive forces overtaking the organization, causing it to either function poorly or fail. This was certainly the case with WorldCom. At first, this company was driven to be the best in its industry. Employees believed in the company and what it stood for, but its leaders let them down. They acted in ways that were contrary to the values, and their greed began to eat away at the core values. The contradictions overcame the company's goal of being the best.

At different points in time, an organization or an individual may choose to emphasize certain values over others. There can be more or less emphasis placed on certain things. For example, at one point American Express had six stated values. Its leaders decided that two more values were very important, so it added those two to its official values statement. In 2004, the Florida Department of Transportation had five stated values and then deleted one. Since then, it has emphasized the remaining four values in its history and development.

Organizational Vision and Personal Vision

Individuals also have motivating visions, many of which are personal. These address what the individuals want to get out of life and how they expect to carry out their lives. It is important to have a personal vision because it gives meaning to life; it directs behavior and mobilizes energy. One personal vision is about what work ought to be like. This is framed over time, based on early experiences, so by the time a person has attained work maturity, the personal vision is pretty clear. However, such a vision can change. For example, a vision might change based on an extremely positive or negative emotional experience at work. This could be something such as a massive layoff or a job change that required the person to move from one end of the country to another.

What is most important about an individual's vision is that it be totally meaningful, based on where the person is in life, what he or she wants to do and/or attain, and how he or she wants to get there. Furthermore, if people are to be contented (or even effective) in their work, it is important that their personal visions of what work should be are congruent with the visions of their organization. In other words, the organization's vision and the person's vision of work need to be aligned. In order to maximize such things as productivity, quality, and service, it is important for the person's vision and the organization's vision to be maximally aligned. As alignment increases, all else being equal, we are most likely to see more positive results. These results are what the individual and the organization desire.

Organizational Values and Personal Values

Values congruence is a derivative of vision congruence in many ways and, on the other hand, values support and enhance the vision.

Organizational values and individual values are separate things that may change over time. But if a person remains with an organization, there usually is a set of shared values. When an individual's and an organization's values are congruent, there is an excitement or energy generated for the individual. The organization generates as much excitement and/or energy in its employees as it does values congruence. When employees perceive that they and the organization stand for the same things, they have deep feelings for things such as loyalty, integrity, teamwork, and service—or whatever the organization's values are. This is why it is very important for an organization to seek employees (especially in the higher levels) who have the same values as the organization.

Ways To Enhance Values Congruence

Many organizations make every effort to hire people who share their values. When this happens successfully, an organization creates a situation in which greater results for the individuals and the organization can be commonplace. Of course, sometimes it is difficult to determine just what a prospective employee believes in. It also can be difficult for an organization to keep individual and organizational values in alignment, because the organization's values can change and an individual's values can change.

An organization can choose to do nothing and hope for the best or it can take the opportunity to enhance and create greater values congruence as often as possible by using various approaches. These approaches include specific strategies and tools that organizations can use.

7

Behavioral Interviewing

Hiring people who hold values that are aligned with the values of the organization can be helped by the use of behavioral-interviewing techniques. This approach is based on asking questions about 1) previous, successful work behaviors and 2) how the candidate might behave in situations in the new job. The interviewer must be clear about what the prospective employee's job content would be and how it relates to each of the organization's values. He or she can then ask questions that are designed to elicit information about how the employee would be likely to act on the job in specific situations and then evaluate the responses in relation to the organization's values. For example, the interviewer might say, "Describe a time in your current job that required you to be a successful team player," or "What have you done to satisfy a very upset customer?"

Communicating the Values Repeatedly to Employees

Organizations should communicate their values and the behavioral expectations that go along with those values to their employees. It is important that this first be done during new-employee orientation programs. It also must be done on a continuing basis. Values can be communicated through staff meetings, the company newsletter, bulletin boards, the company website, the back of business cards, during performance appraisals, and through company-sponsored training programs that leaders and employees attend.

When I did executive-development training for a company a few years ago, the executives wanted to make sure that all the content in the training program was related to one of the organization's values.

It is important to note that some sets of values also can be communicated through training programs that employees attend that are not sponsored by the organization, such as those presented through training organizations and in different parts of the country and the world. Some of these may conflict with the organization's values. This may or may not be a good thing. It can be good if the returning employees feel free to discuss them so that the "new" values can be examined. If they are deemed worthy of adoption by the organization, it can take appropriate steps to integrate the new values into the organizational culture.

In the old days, people sat around a fire and told stories. Today, we tell stories everywhere. Storytelling is a very valuable tool, not just for education but also for providing examples of employee actions that are congruent with the organization's values. My students believe that hearing organizational stories enhances their understanding of the organization's values and expectations. They often talk about using a story at the beginning of a meeting to illustrate how a particular employee supported a value in a special way.

Walking the Talk

The most important way to communicate values is to live them—what is called "walking the talk." Leaders in organizations

9

must learn the values and the accompanying behavioral expectations and must make them clear in their dealings with all employees. "This is what we expect from people" must be modeled in the leaders' behaviors.

Teaching Leaders

As experience over the centuries has proved, one of the most important responsibilities of leaders is to teach other leaders. However, how to do it well may not be as clear as the fact that it needs to be done. Leadership-development specialists, consultants, and executives all have tried a wide variety of approaches to teaching leadership. My students believe that the best way to teach leadership is through example. Leaders need to behave in ways that they expect the next generation of leaders to behave and they need to explain why they behave that way.

Reinforcing Standards and Expectations

Another way to enhance values congruence is by establishing consequences of behavior so that standards and expectations are enforced. This means using positive and negative reinforcement. This requires diligent effort on the part of leaders. They need to continually be in touch with employees and observe them carefully. Such observation will enable leaders to deliver the appropriate rewards or negative reinforcement based on the exact behavior of individual employees.

Allocating Resources To Support the Values

An organization's values are enhanced when the allocation of resources is consistent with the values of the organization. For example, if customer satisfaction is important, the organization needs to make resources available to people so that they can provide customers with positive experiences. If an organization says that its human resources are valuable, the organization must spend the money needed to retain outstanding employees. If an organization feels that quality of products and services is a key to its strategy for success, it must provide the resources to create and deliver quality products and services. In order to enhance values congruence, it is essential to allocate the resources needed to support the organization's values.

Periodically Assessing the Organization

Another important way to enhance organizational values is to conduct a periodic evaluation of the organization's values. For example, it was not that long ago that lists of corporate values did not include such things as racial equality, diversity, team building, encouraging employees to see how their work makes a contribution, innovation, learning from mistakes, strategic planning, and an emphasis on customer service. Many organizations emphasize these things now. The point is that the values that organizations choose to emphasize can change.

Just as organizations need to do periodic evaluations, individuals may be doing something similar. I remember waking up one morning

11

and realizing that my personal values had changed and that they were a lot different from the values that the organization I worked for espoused. It was natural for me to decide to leave the organization. The important point is to evaluate whether the currently stated values are what the organization actually wants to emphasize and what the individual wants to emphasize.

It is difficult to overemphasize the importance of being consistent as a way to enhance values. There are many opportunities to behave in accordance with values, and there also are situations in which employees may be lured into behaviors that are contrary to the values of the organization. Organizations and individuals must resist efforts and temptations that would have them behave in ways that are inconsistent with their stated values.

Conclusion

There are many people who believe that it is important to be passionate about what you do, where you do it, why you do it, when you do it, and with whom you do it. However, there may be something even more important—something deeper. As an analogy, the deeper place inside a human is in the bone marrow. The head, the heart, and the body all depend on the bone marrow. Congruence between vision and values is like bone marrow in enabling successful leadership.

Personal Assessment of Vision and Values Congruence

Questions for Reflection

1. Have the vision and values of the organization been communicated to all employees?

2. To what extent do you think the values support the vision?

3. What actions do leaders take in your organization to reinforce the values?

4. What role do you need to play in developing vision and values congruence?

Personal Actions

1. Description of what you did:

2. Were any resources required?

3. How were you able to sustain the effort?

4. Description of how people reacted:

5. What about the people who did not react?

6. How creative were you?

7. Quantitative assessment of what you did: What was the impact?

8. How did you know what the impact was?

9. Ways to spread this best practice:

10. What is the possible long-term impact?

11. What is the payback to you?

Chapter 2

Link Strategic Elements

When I was growing up, my family drove around town from time to time. During these trips, I noted that it seemed as though every time a fast-food restaurant was built, shortly thereafter its competition built one, too. Finally, I asked my business education teacher in high school what was going on. Mr. Webb answered with one word: "Strategy." He explained that it was the strategy of fast-food restaurants during those times to be where other fast food restaurants were. He said that it took a lot of people to build a store. First, someone had to identify a good site. Next, someone had to get permits to build the store and buy equipment. A manager had to be hired, and the manager had to hire people and train them. All the people had to work together to make the "strategy" work, just as in an athletic team. I realized that someone was making sure that all the elements of the strategy were linked in some way.

Linking strategic elements means that all elements of an organization's strategic plan are interdependent. No strategic element stands by itself. All the elements and the organizational functions are simultaneously providing inputs and outputs to one another.

Linking strategic elements can be a very difficult job for leaders. Many different parts of an organization may seem to be in competition. People do not always cooperate even when the goal to improve business results is driving everybody in the organization. However, the most successful organizations have found ways to lessen the conflict and link the strategic elements in ways that enable more successful business results than those that are obtained by organizations that are not able to link their strategic elements.

Thinking Strategically

The beginning of this process is being able to think strategically. Thinking strategically means opening your thinking to possibilities. Effective leaders light the fires of strategic thinking by bringing together all the people in the organization that need to be involved in linking the strategic elements. This includes representatives from all necessary functions and levels of the organization. For example, functions might include accounting, finance, human resources, marketing, and operations. "Levels of the organization" refers to line employees, first-level supervisors, middle managers, senior managers, and executives. If the organization's approach to leading and managing is exclusionary, the group will be smaller. If it is inclusionary, the process may even include some vendors, customers, and regulators.

Next, the leaders clearly communicate what the organization's goals are. They focus on what they would like to do (as opposed to focusing on people, finances, technology, or other resource issues that are going to be addressed). Then they ask a wide variety of questions to stimulate people's thinking. Finally, they elicit all the ideas they possibly can get.

In this process, the people sitting around the table have come prepared. They know where the highs and lows of knowledge and skill are in the work force, based on the skills-inventory database managed by human resources. They also know how well different levels and functions in the organization have used best practices, from inside and outside the organization. They know the levels of productivity and quality. They know about the work climate. They know about cost control. They know what their customers think of the products or services they provide.

The fire is lit by asking questions. Everyone needs to respond to the questions. This allows the facilitator of the strategic-thinking process to identify how well the different organizational functions and levels are linked already. The facilitator may be an experienced consultant or one of the leaders of the organization. Some of the things to be asked are:

1. What is today's most important issue and what will tomorrow's be?
2. What are we most and least proud of?
3. What should we be doing that we are not doing?
4. How are we doing in terms of our internal customers?
5. How are we doing in terms of our external customers?
6. What can we learn from outside the organization (including from our vendors and competitors)?

7. What do we do that is different and special in our organization?

8. How well do we use our financial resources?

9. How well do we use our technological resources?

10. How well do we use our human resources?

11. Do we need to review our vision and/or our mission (both organization wide and departmental)?

12. Why do people choose to work here?

13. What is it that we stand for; what are our values?

To prepare for linking the strategic elements, an organization needs to develop a set of criteria unique to that organization. It could include some of the following:

1. Knowing that leadership is more effective when it uses planning as a process to lead the organization forward.

2. Using the communication system to let people know what the strategy is.

3. Nudging people to think about the long term—about the impact of what they do.

4. Knowing about the economy, the marketplace, the competition, and the possible future competition.

5. Allowing enough time for planning and for people to work on linking their pieces of the strategic plan together.

6. Staying flexible.

7. Making sure that top management is involved in the process and speaks openly about the process and its results.

8. Making sure that quantifiable analysis and resource allocation are withheld until everything that needs to be thought about and evaluated has been identified.

Once the linking criteria are identified (whatever they are for a particular organization), it is important to know the extent to which they exist in the organization. This entails assessing each criterion to determine if it occurs all the time, some of the time, rarely, or never. By doing this, leaders increase their own understanding, and the people who are responsible for thinking strategically and linking strategic elements are better prepared to move forward.

Goal Analysis

As leaders begin to link strategic elements, they must also do some goal analysis. They must access organizational goals, departmental goals, individual work-unit goals, and individual goals. For each of these four areas, long-term and short-term goals must be identified and analyzed. Unless there is analysis, there can be no determination of how strong the links are. The results of the analysis may suggest that the links are weak or strong or somewhere in between. The important outcome is that the people who are involved are aware of the information as they determine how they are going to link all the elements of the strategy.

To assist in the goal analysis, some questions can be asked. These questions can cause people to think more deeply about goals, connecting the goals, the overall strategy, and the linkages among the strategic elements. The questions are as follows:

1. Which goals have been given the highest priority and by whom?
2. Which goals need to have higher priority, according to whom?
3. To what extent are organizational, departmental, work-unit, and individual goals aligned? (This is an important, thought-provoking question because the amount of linkage that is present or desired becomes apparent to everyone.)
4. How should we allocate resources among the goals?
5. Should long-term or short-term goals receive more attention from the organization, departments, work units, and individuals?
6. How often should we assess to determine the alignment or the linkages?
7. As the goals are reviewed, does it become evident that some of the goals may need to be revised?
8. Are there any goals that are difficult to obtain or more difficult than others to obtain?
9. Which goals seem the easiest to obtain for the organization, departments, work units, and individuals?

Thinking strategically includes making sure that the organization's vision and mission statements are reviewed continually. When that is done, all the functions in the organization must be informed of any changes so that everyone who speaks with a department or work unit is clear about what needs to be linked.

In linking strategic elements, leaders establish an environment for obtaining excellent business results. This is a result of conscious effort, and conscious effort can be identified as proceeding along one or more paths. These paths include: the productivity path, the quality path, the service path, the cost-control path, and the uniqueness path. These paths must be assessed from the current and future perspectives. Which leaders, departments, work units, and individuals are on which path? Are these paths aligned and linked now and how will they be in the future? "Linked" refers to interdependences; "aligned" refers to agreement on the work products of those linkages.

Examining Results

One important thing to keep in mind is that individuals may need the most help with this. Individuals can be asked to list their major outputs or the results they are required to produce, and these results can be prioritized in bundles. This means placing each priority in one of three categories: high, medium, or low. In so doing, the individual can consider the following questions:

1. Who needs this output?
2. How is the output delivered to the people who need it?
3. How do I measure the extent to which that output has been attained?
4. How do I measure how satisfied the receivers of that output are?
5. Is this a continuing output or an output that is sporadic or one will be gone as soon as I am finished?

The development of a relationship with the receivers of the output is necessary. Their perspective on the quality and service of the output is very important. It is important to consider how much more of the output the individual or the work unit could provide. Knowledge of what the receivers of the output value also is important. For example, would they prefer quality over timeliness or timeliness over quality? Other essential things to know about the users are: How much of what we are providing do they need? Are there any differences in the amounts required? Are the users increasing or declining in number? How is technology related to providing the particular output? In what direction is the technology headed? Do the users' needs occur at the beginning or end of the business cycle or year?

Up to this point it is easy to surmise that all this strategic analysis is helping us to build linkages. The linkages are like circles all touching one another. We are talking about high levels of relatedness or, better, total relatedness or, even better, interrelatedness. The linkages are based on sequential or pooled interdependences of work products. All input/output relationships are created by those interdependences.

Doing Gap Analysis

Whenever analysis occurs, problems and opportunities are uncovered. Gaps between what is desired and what exists may appear. It is necessary to know how important it is to eliminate any gap. If a gap must be closed, how is that to be done? What resources might be required to close the gap?

22

Gap Analysis

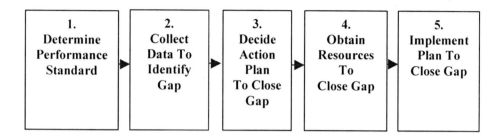

Step 1. This step requires that a precise standard or expectation be identified. This will be a technological, financial, or human standard of performance. An approach for measuring the performance also should be identified in this step and should include time frames.

Step 2. Data is collected in this step to see if the actual performance was consistent with the expected performance. If there is no gap, no further action is required. If there is a gap, a plan must be developed to close the gap. If the gap is not considered worth closing, nothing else is done until the next round of data collection.

Step 3. Ultimately, a plan must be implemented to eliminate the gap. The plan should be developed by the person who has primary accountability for closing the gap. The plan must include the action steps, identification of who is responsible for each step, time lines, and resource requirements.

Step 4. This is a critical step. Regardless of the type and amount of resources, they must be nailed down. This is a major concern. The gap can be eliminated only if the necessary resources are available.

Step 5. Implementing the plan to eliminate the gap is the end of the line—at least until another data collection reveals that a gap still exists. The implementation requires close monitoring of the plans, time lines, and resources utilization.

SWOT

Inherent in everything discussed so far is the popular strategic-planning tool called SWOT. SWOT stands for *strengths, weaknesses, opportunities,* and *threats.* During a strategic-planning exercise, there may be a formal portion of the process when SWOT is used. Strengths, weaknesses, opportunities, and threats are part of all the strategic-thinking tools, perspectives, and questions that have been presented.

Contingency Thinking

Another issue to consider when it comes to linking strategic elements is contingency thinking. We can have all the elements linked together perfectly, but what if we have the wrong perspective for some of the elements? It is essential to have a contingency position. Most leaders do not spend a lot of time on contingency thinking, but there are some advantages to including it. The first is knowing what the deviance possibilities are for each of the links of the strategy. For example, if the plan is to build a plant in a different part of the world and assume that everyone will want to work in the plant, what happens if it is not possible to hire enough people to work there? Other aspects of contingency

24

thinking include knowing how well the organization, departments, individual work units, and individuals are functioning. Leaders also need to know what potential budget variations may occur on either the revenue side or the expense side. What will the possible responses be if there are variations? Lastly, leaders should know about resources, services requirements, etc., if strategies begin to be impractical as the organization makes itself ready for a new direction.

Knowledge Management

In linking strategic elements, a very powerful function must be accounted for: knowledge management. Individual departments and work units can be held responsible for knowledge management. There can be an organization-wide knowledge-management function. The purpose is to collect and disseminate the knowledge that has taken the organization to where it is and that can take it to where it wants to go. Organizational knowledge can be stored electronically.

In order to link all strategic elements of an organization, it is necessary to know how people in each department and in each work unit share information and knowledge with one another, within the work unit or department, and with other work units or departments across the organization. It is important that the organization be aware of what new knowledge needs to exist throughout the organization and/or in individual departments and work units. It is equally important that the organization prevent redundancy; there is no need for different parts of the organization to reinvent knowledge. The organization needs to know where new knowledge will come from; how the knowledge will be stored, accessed, and disseminated; and how the knowledge-management efforts will be evaluated.

Leadership Cooperation

The bottom line for linking strategic elements is that all leaders must cooperate in providing information, sharing knowledge, and keeping an eye on the long term. Leaders must work together as a team, even though this is often difficult at the highest levels in an organization. The linking of strategic elements can lead to greater focus, timely action, and the results that are expected. As many people as possible must be engaged in linking strategic elements. Throughout the organization, people must know and understand their roles in keeping the links strong but flexible.

Personal Assessment of Linking Strategic Elements

Questions for Reflection

1. What is the purpose of linking strategic elements?

2. How well does each employee in your organization understand his/her role in linking strategic elements?

3. In what ways would you improve your efforts in linking strategic elements?

4. What best practices in strategic planning are you aware of that your organization could adopt?

Personal Actions

1. Description of what you did:

2. Were any resources required?

3. How were you able to sustain the effort?

4. Description of how people reacted:

5. What about the people who did not react?

6. How creative were you?

7. Quantitative assessment of what you did: What was the impact?

8. How did you know what the impact was?

9. Ways to spread this best practice:

10. What is the possible long-term impact?

11. What is the status now? Are things still progressing?

Chapter 3

Decision Making on the Leadership Road

When I was in high school, I asked one of my favorite teachers, Mr. Dominic, what he thought about me going to business school in college. His quick response was that it was not a good idea for me to go to business school because I changed my mind all the time. I asked him what he meant by that, and he said that only the previous week, I had asked him if I would be a good teacher. He knew that my decision-making capabilities needed some development.

That encounter taught me the importance of weighing all the options before making a decision. I was prone to making decisions too quickly, without as much information as I needed. I resolved to get as much information as I reasonably could before making an important decision in the future.

Adding Value

A colleague of mine once said that leadership is just one darn thing after another. I think he meant that leaders have to make decisions continually. They make decisions about small and large issues. They make decisions that will have short-term and long-term impacts. The most important thing for leaders to keep in mind is that their decisions must add value.

Leaders must make decisions based on their knowledge, how fast they learn, and how adaptable they are. They add value by taking the organization to a new level, some place it has not been before. They add value by redirecting the organization. What matters is that the value of the organization is higher than it was before the decision was made. It may be higher in financial value or stature in the community. It may be in a better position to weather economic downturns.

An effective leader distinguishes himself or herself from ineffective leaders by making wise decisions about the things that count in an organization. These include productivity, quality, service, and cost avoidance. The best decisions are related to one or all of these four items. Therefore, a leader needs to ensure that the decisions that are made for the organization have been thoroughly assessed before they are finalized. This means that leaders must be clear about the perspectives, approaches, and tools that they and others use. Leaders must see the nature of the value they add in making decisions.

Perspectives, Approaches, and Tools

Leaders' decisions are influenced by their perspectives, approaches, and tools. The perspectives that leaders have are the results of their previous decision-making experiences and how well those turned out.

Their perspectives also are based on their personal styles and the values that they believe are important at that time in the organization. Remember that values are those things that leaders are willing to act on consistently after considering options and the consequences of those options.

Leaders have different approaches to making decisions. Some make decisions in line with the philosophy of the Lone Ranger—by themselves, without any input from anyone else. At the other extreme are the leaders who delegate all decision making to subordinates. In between are the leaders who make decisions after the people who have appropriate information have discussed the information and made recommendations about what the most appropriate decisions would be. Another approach to decision making is one in which the leaders ask experts inside their organizations to provide information about particular decision-making situations and then make the decisions themselves.

Tools are devices that leaders use in the decision-making process. Perhaps the best example of such a tool is a decision matrix. A decision matrix involves identifying criteria for making the decision. Then it often is important to identify as many feasible options as possible. This can be done using the tool of brainstorming. The next step is to list the criteria for making the decision along the top boxes of a 5 x 5 matrix. The options are listed separately in each box down the left side. Each criterion is assessed against each option using a point system. The scores are totaled horizontally to identify the best possible option.

Ensuring That Decisions Are Implemented

Leaders distinguish themselves by making decisions that are considered successful to objective observers. The most important thing a leader can do in terms of decision making is to ensure implementation. It is one thing to say that you are going to bring a new product to market on January 15, but it is quite another thing to make it happen by January 15. There are some actions that leaders can take to ensure that their decisions are implemented.

1. Assume that all information was available during the decision making—that all the experts who contributed the appropriate information have done their jobs well. However, if new information arises that makes the validity of the decision questionable, it probably is a good idea to put the implementation on hold and reconsider the game plan.

2. Be sure that the accounting and legal departments have given their approval to the decision and implementation plan. There are many laws that govern how businesses, governments, non-profit organizations, and educational institutions are run. The accounting and legal departments need to be consulted, and their advice should be followed. (Make sure that their approval is obtained in writing.)

3. Make sure that you have full support from the CEO (unless it is the CEO who made the decision). This means obtaining a public statement from the CEO supporting the decision and the implementation plan. It means having the CEO support the

decision in appropriate public appearances. The CEO must do whatever it takes to drive home how important the decision is to the organization. If the organization is dispersed across a wide geographical area or if the decision will affect only those lower down on the organizational chart, another key person must make sure that everyone knows that there is top support for the decision.

4. Leaders should inform all appropriate parties before moving forward. These parties could include the members of the board of directors, key leaders, customers, vendors, managers, and employees. All stakeholder groups that will be affected by the decision should be informed of the decision, the implementation plan, and the expected results.

5. The leader must identify the best time to announce the decision. He or she must assess what else is going on in the organization and in its external environment. For example, what information is going to be released by an industry group or by the government? The decision should be announced when one can get the full attention of the people. The leader also should identify the best place in which, or the best means by which, to announce the decision. It may be announced in the boardroom or at a social event. It may be announced by e-mail. The leader must assess what the best approach is, based on his or her understanding of the organization and its culture.

6. The leader should inform everyone that the decision is acceptable, whether he or she makes it or someone else makes it. It is

important to state that numerous perspectives were taken into account and that this was the best possible decision that could have been made, given the available resources.

7. Leaders must deal assertively with challenges to their decisions. These usually come from people who disagree because of their perspectives. They may think that a decision is not in their best interests or the best interests of the organization. They also may be people who disagree merely because they typically disagree.

8. A leader needs to quickly obtain or reserve the needed re-sources. Making sure that they are available in order to move forward is very important. A resource may be new financing. It may be a special kind of retention strategy or a group of key people who will be involved in carrying out the decision. What-ever resources are needed, they must be obtained quickly so that people can take action.

9. Determine associated training needs and implement necessary training programs. Often, decisions require that people gain new knowledge, new skills, or new attitudes. People in the organiza-tion may need to be trained immediately to facilitate rapid implementation of the plan. A change in resource utilization also may be a reason for new training.

10. Leaders must overcome procrastination. They need to short cir-cuit second-guessing. They need to keep the focus and the energy on moving forward. When there is momentum in im-plementation, there is not as much likelihood of procrastination and second-guessing.

11. Operationalize the plan that was developed to implement the decision. Implementation is the total package of fourteen actions, while operationalization is just putting the plan into operation.

12. A leader needs to take a positive view of all tasks to be performed as part of the implementation. Moving forward one step at a time is preferable to taking two steps forward and one step back. Of course, it is possible that some variable or information from an outside source may confound a decision and that adjustments will have to be made. Generally, however, all the tasks that have been identified as part of the implementation must be viewed positively and optimistically.

13. Use change-management tactics to move things along. (Chapter 5 discusses change management.) Proven change-management tactics and tools can be very helpful in implementing decisions.

14. Leaders need to clarify their expectations about follow-through requirements. Follow-through requirements include time lines. These can be represented by a Gantt chart or a PERT chart or software that allows time lines to be established and tracked. Other expectations may be about allocations of financial, human, and technological resources. Whatever a leader has in mind regarding the outcome of a decision, it needs to be clearly described and disseminated to those who are involved in implementing that decision.

Personal Assessment of Decision Making

Questions for Reflection

1. How would you describe the approach to decision making in your organization?

2. How are the impacts of decisions measured?

3. Describe the system that monitors decision follow-up in your organization.

4. How skilled do you personally feel in making decisions?

Personal Actions

1. Description of what you did in terms of a major decision:

2. Were any resources required?

3. How were you able to sustain the effort?

4. Description of how people reacted:

5. What about the people who did not react?

6. Quantitative assessment of what you did: What was the impact?

7. How did you know what the impact was?

8. Ways to spread this best practice:

9. What is the possible long-term impact?

10. What is the payback to you?

11. What is the status now? Are things still progressing?

Chapter 4

Create an Atmosphere for Open Communication

When I was growing up, I could talk to anybody in my family, any time, about anything. I lived with my mother and father, and my grandmother lived in a house right behind us. My grandfather created an atmosphere of open communication. I saw my cousins from New York in the summers, and we talked a lot. It is apparent to me that the most important aspect of communication in my family is that whatever people say is accepted as their way of expressing themselves. There was feedback, but it was never belittling, chastising, or abusive. Everyone was accepted as a person with something important to say.

When I began to work while in high school, it became clear that communication with others could be different from what I had experienced at home. Later, I worked in some organizations in which everyone communicated openly. I also worked in some organizations in which people had to be very careful about what they said, to whom they said it, when they said it, and even where they said it.

Elements of Open Communication

Leaders deal with a basic communication process each day. The communication process is very simple: first somebody identifies the need for a message to be sent. It can be delivered face to face, over the telephone, in written form, or by e-mail. Second, the message is coded, which means that someone makes a decision about what to say and how to say it. Third, the message is sent. Next, the message is received; someone hears it or sees it. Fifth, the message is decoded; that is, it is interpreted by the receiver. Usually this happens simply and quickly. However, the process can go awry if the sender does not speak or write clearly or if he or she uses terms (such as jargon) that the receiver does not understand. Normally, the last step is that feedback is provided. The feedback is reverse communication, back to the sender. This completes the communication process.

The following are some basic practices that help to establish an environment in which open communication thrives. Some of them are explained more fully in the sections that follow.

1. Show respect to the other person.
2. Ask the other person what he or she thinks.
3. Ask rather than tell, except in an emergency.
4. Imagine yourself in the other person's situation.
5. Give the other person's needs equal priority.
6. Emphasize the importance of businesslike communication.

7. Be positive in your communications. (It is a known fact that the best leaders are optimistic.)

8. Say "please" and "thank you" as much as you can.

9. Avoid communication stoppers—words and behaviors that have a negative impact. Examples are interrupting, putting people down, ignoring people, being distracted, arguing, blaming, labeling, lecturing, attempting to control, attacking, giving unsolicited advice, and commanding. One of the most famous of all communication stoppers is "Yes, but."

10. Do not say anything that might hurt the other person's self-esteem.

11. Listen carefully and listen for feelings behind the words.

12. Always give all your attention (with your face and your body language) to the person with whom you are communicating.

13. Indicate that you are paying attention. Use reinforcement, such as nodding.

14. Watch the other person's body language, which can give you clues as to the person's levels of understanding, comfort, etc.

15. Try to head off any problems you think may be about to develop.

Of course, there are more sophisticated elements of open communication. The most successful leaders understand and make use of these in their day-to-day dealings with others.

Identifying Communication Styles

One of the more important points when it comes to leaders establishing an environment of open communication is the ability and willingness to communicate to different people in different ways. People communicate differently because they have different styles, based on their personalities, cultural backgrounds, attitudes about the message, and moods.

One of the most popular ways of understanding how people communicate has to do with how they process information. In the Neurolinguistic Programming model of communication, people are said to process information in three different modes: visual, auditory, and kinesthetic. People who are primarily visual tend to say things such as, "I see the pattern now" and "That looks like a good idea." They usually speak with a fast tempo. People who are primarily auditory might say things such as, "I hear you" and "That rings a bell." These people typically do not speak as rapidly as the people who have a visual style. The third mode is the kinesthetic, or physical. People who are primarily kinesthetic are likely to say things such as, "I can't get a handle on it" and "Walk me through it." These people often speak in a slow tempo with long pauses.

A skilled communicator learns how to speak in the style of the person with whom he or she is communicating. If you want to have an open communication environment, you need to be able to use different styles in order to make others feel comfortable and to encourage their communication.

Speaking to Others As Equals

Leaders who are good at building openness in the communication process maintain open minds. They listen to anything from anyone at almost any time, unless it becomes clear that the communication is not adding value.

Speaking to others as equals is of monumental importance. Although organizational charts place some people in positions that have more authority and responsibility, this does not mean that others are of lesser importance. An effective leader speaks to other people as if they were his or her peers. "Talking down" to people will immediately affect the communication in a negative way and may shut it off. Even during periods of organizational crisis, when you may be required to make an authoritarian decision, it is not appropriate to talk down to people.

Being Clear

Another consideration in establishing an open communication environment is to make sure that your communication is understood. It is important to speak clearly and distinctly. In many cases, it is necessary to avoid jargon and to use short words and sentences. It is especially important that a leader leave no doubt about what he or she is saying. Remember that communication is a two-way transaction. People should always have an opportunity to respond or to provide feedback. It often helps to ask the other person if he or she has any comments or questions. If you merely ask, "Do you understand?" the person almost always will say, "Yes" in order not to appear to be dense.

Giving Feedback Appropriately

Open communication requires an opportunity for feedback. Effective feedback is purposeful, and leaders who are good at providing feedback do certain things:

1. They consider the other person's perspective.
2. They provide specific, descriptive feedback that can be acted on. For example, rather than saying, "Your work isn't good," a leader might say, "The last two XY parts were four days late, and this is not acceptable." Rather than saying, "You aren't making sense," a leader might say, "I don't understand what you mean about the vendor causing the problem; can you rephrase that part?"
3. They provide descriptive, rather than evaluative, feedback. For example, one would say, "The part being late caused a problem with production" rather than "You're lazy."
4. They do not distort the feedback, e.g., "You are always late" or "You never get work in on time".
5. They record the feedback when appropriate.
6. They are clear about why they are giving the feedback. For example, "I need to ensure that the project deadline is met" or "You will need to explain this problem more clearly in the meeting on Tuesday, and I didn't understand what you were saying when you first described it to me."

7. They provide the feedback at the appropriate time—usually as soon as possible following the communication or behavior to which the feedback is a response. Saving negative feedback for one big dump truck unloading really harms the communication environment, and by then it may be too late for the person to do anything about the problem. Similarly, it is important to give positive feedback as soon as possible in order to reinforce the desired behavior.

Delivering Bad News Effectively

From time to time it is necessary for a leader to deliver bad news. This could mean telling someone that her idea may not have as much impact as she thought or telling someone that he's not going to receive the promotion he thought he would receive. To keep the open-communication environment, it is important to deliver bad news in a way that helps people to accept it better. This is never easy, but there are some things that can help.

1. Ensure privacy. Deliver bad news to the person who needs to hear the bad news and only that person. Close the door. This means that cubicles are not good places in which to deliver bad news.

2. Ensure freedom from interruptions. Notify your secretary or assistant to hold your calls. If the telephone rings, do not interrupt the conversation to answer it.

3. Stay focused on the issue. Beating around the bush or wandering aimlessly during the conversation only makes it worse for the person receiving the bad news.

45

4. Maintain a businesslike approach. This is not a time to try to be friendly or provide warm fuzzies. This does not mean that you should be cold or insensitive; it means that you should remain businesslike. Stay in control of the discussion. Present your case with specifics, not generalities. Let the other person know exactly what the news is and what the reason for it is. Do not allow the discussion to get into personality issues.

5. Avoid trying to soft-peddle or sweeten the negative stuff. It is what it is.

6. If the person has made a mistake, do not rub it in. Ask the person if there is anything that he or she needs help with. Listen carefully to the person's response and pay attention to his or her nonverbal communication.

Following Through

Follow-through often is essential. Although it may not be necessary all the time, it is important for a leader to be able to identify when follow-through is necessary and when it is not. The need for follow-through may be immediate or it may occur at some time in the future. Follow-through keeps communication channels open. Also, if you doubt that your message has been received positively, you can follow up later to make sure that it has been understood or that people are taking the necessary action.

Supportive Communication

Another way of looking at communication was popularized by Jack Gibb: supportive versus defensive communication. People who communicate supportively do so in a positive way that contributes to an open-communication environment. They speak in an objective, clear, and fair manner. They try to approach things from a mutual problem-solving perspective. They understand that both people's perspectives are important in the communication and they encourage honest expression of ideas. You can tell that such persons have respect for those with whom they are communicating. The bottom line is that during supportive communication, people are flexible and open minded.

Defensive communication, on the other hand, usually leads to the communication being cut off prematurely. A defensive communicator speaks in a critical and/or judgmental way, whether it be in person, over the telephone, in writing, or by e-mail. People who throw up defensive communication barriers often speak as if they are the only experts. They tend to be inflexible. They know everything, they have an answer for everything, and typically try to twist the facts or reinterpret the facts to back up their positions. They try to manipulate the conversations in this and other ways. Often, they are aloof and/or condescending—speaking as if they are better than the people with whom they are communicating. In the long run—if not in the short run—their style fails, because the person on the other end of the communication clams up or becomes aggressive.

Communicating Across Generations

I'm not convinced that there is huge communication gap between generations, but it certainly helps a leader to understand the languages of other generations so that he or she can speak in ways that they understand (e.g., use examples that make sense to them). Here are some tips for dealing with people from generations other than one's own:

1. Let the person talk about his or her past experiences.
2. Ask for examples of what the person is saying.
3. Be willing to repeat things, especially questions. The other person may not be tuned in to the way you think or the way you express yourself or your view of things.
4. With older people, connect the past to the present situation.
5. Help older people with new communication technology.
6. Coach younger people on their communication skills, if needed.

Selling Ideas

The final thing to keep in mind when trying to maintain an open-communication environment is to sell your ideas and let other people sell their ideas. To sell your ideas, you must do the following:

1. Plan. You need to know everything about the idea you are selling and when to sell it.
2. Expect to succeed. Be confident and enthusiastic.
3. Make sure that others are clear from the beginning about what your purpose is.

4. Make sure you have people's attention. Choose your time and place.

5. Get your key points out on the table. Present a balanced picture of the idea you are trying to get across. Show how the benefits outweigh the disadvantages.

6. Be brief.

7. Get the listeners involved.

8. As you conclude, ask for what you would like to have from the person you are attempting to sell your idea to. Get the person to agree on a plan.

9. Follow up. If your idea isn't sold, decide how to overcome the resistance. Keep trying.

Personal Assessment of Open Communication

Questions for Reflection

1. How would you assess the level of open communication in your organization?

2. How well do you and other people in your organization give feedback?

3. How good are you and other people in your organization at delivering bad news?

4. How much more do you need to know about communicating across generations?

5. How well do you and other people in your organization sell their ideas to others?

Personal Actions

1. Description of what you did:

2. Description of how people reacted:

3. What about the people who didn't react?

4. How creative were you?

5. Quantitative assessment of what you did: What was the impact?

6. How did you know what the impact was?

7. What are ways to spread this best practice?

8. What's the payback to you?

Chapter 5

Lead for Change

I was ten when my parents made a major move from one part of town to another. I had a health problem shortly after that. The doctor concluded that I was just unhappy about moving across town. It wasn't serious but, as a father, I made sure that changes that affected my children weren't abrupt or disruptive. I did some things that made it easy for my daughters to adjust; for example, they got to choose the colors of the walls and carpets in their bedrooms. They were involved in discussing what colors the tiles and fixtures would be in the bathroom they would share. I made sure that they got to see some of their old friends. No transition is perfect, but it was less disruptive than my youthful change had been.

Many changes are required in organizations in order to keep up with markets, changing external environments, customers, and other stakeholder demands. Every leader has a responsibility to make sure that when his or her organization changes, it's not disruptive. The leader must have a commitment to managing change. A leader must take a major role in the process or leave the change to other people or to chance. If there are competent internal or external change agents making things happen, the leader need not direct all aspects of the change, but he or she must be involved.

Elements of Organizational Change

My students compiled a list of things that are necessary if organizational change is to be accomplished smoothly. They are presented in the rest of this paragraph. Perhaps one of the most important things is that the leader must get involved in the change. Otherwise people will tend to blow it off and not worry about the adjustments that are required. The leader should make sure that a well-known, well-respected, and well-liked internal executive who is a champion for the change is guiding the process. The leader must communicate continually and consistently about what's happening in terms of the change. If the schedule changes and a timetable will be adjusted, the leader needs to let people know how and why. The leaders also should make sure that time, money, staff, technologies, and other resources are allocated to the direction that the leader is trying to take the organization in the future. Finally, leaders must constantly talk and walk the talk because all actions communicate.

However much the leader chooses to be involved, there are some initial issues that he or she must make sure are addressed. These are: control or non-control, comfort or anxiety, status quo or disruption, cooperation or resistance, the known or the unknown, stabilized relationships or changed relationships, and unchanged work tasks or changed work tasks.

Control or Non-control

Control or non-control is a very simple issue: what's going to change in people's ability or opportunity to control their work and their work spaces and which things are going to slip away? This issue is important to people. It may be real control or it may be perceived (or "felt") influence. People like to feel that they have influence over what they do in their jobs. If, during a period of change, they feel their influence decrease, they may not be as cooperative with the change. Whenever possible, it is important to help people to feel as if their influence over their jobs will be stable during the change. If it is intended to dip for a short period of time, action must be taken to increase the degree of felt influence as soon as possible.

The leader's responsibility is to identify areas where control will remain the same and areas where control will change, where control will be taken away and where it will be added. This information should be shared directly with all employees so that they are able to assess and plan for how their work will be impacted and maintain a sense of order.

Comfort or Anxiety

What are people's comfort levels regarding the change? How much anxiety is there about this change? The leader needs to know how much comfort and how much anxiety exists so that he or she can take the proper steps to alleviate the anxiety and make people more comfortable.

It is important that the leader identify what makes people feel comfortable about the change. These elements should be positively reinforced. The leader also should find out what specifically is causing anxiety about the change, then the leader should connect the affected people to organizational resources that can play a role in reducing their anxiety.

Status Quo or Disruption

Change can disrupt routines, processes, and even relationships. Leaders need to plan how much of the status quo will remain at any particular point during the change so that the people who work in the organization can be comfortable with some things. The leader needs to assess how much disruption they can tolerate and still be productive. The leader also must communicate the expected level of disruption so that people can work with one another to minimize the impact of the disruption.

Cooperation or Resistance

Some people will cooperate and embrace the change. Others will just go along with it, and some will resist. They may resist mildly or strongly. A leader must know what he or she is dealing with when it comes to cooperation and resistance in the organization. It is necessary for the leader to identify people who are cooperative and those who are resistant. Cooperative employees should be engaged as role models. The leader should meet with the resisters to find out the reasons for their resistance. The leader will then be able to identify what needs to be done to lower the resistance.

The Known or the Unknown

When faced with change, people worry about the unknown. The more unknown there is, the more uncomfortable people will be. The more open and explicit the communication during the period of change, the better. Therefore, the leader's main task is to ensure continual communication. This can be accomplished through all-personnel meetings, department meetings, team meetings, organizational newsletters, and the like.

Stabilized Relationships or Changed Relationships

Creating trouble during change can be as simple as establishing a new procedure that keeps people who have been having coffee together at 10:15 every morning for two years from doing that any more. It can lead to a change in the relationships among those people and can extend to their business relationships. Leaders must make every effort to stabilize and keep relationships in place that are essential for the morale of groups and teams. Creating new relationships can be helpful; however, it should be done along with preserving some or all of the old ones. Leaders can use sociograms to identify existing relationship patterns. This will help them in making choices that affect organizational relationships.

Unchanged Work Tasks or Changed Work Tasks

The leader must determine whether people's work tasks will stay the same or change. This involves assessing how many of them will stay the same, how many of them will change, how difficult it will be for people to learn and get used to the new ways of doing things, and how difficult it will be to give up the old ways. The leader must address such issues. The most important consideration is for the leader to make certain that a training-needs analysis is conducted and that training programs are made available for all who will need them.

Planning the Change

Adequate time must be spent in planning the change. The leader must plan it from a big-picture perspective. There are many issues that the leader must resolve so that he or she can guide people through the change and communicate what they need to do so that they can guide others through the change. The leader should have concrete details about where the organization is going, what it will look like, feel like, and so on. He or she must know what the impact will be on task accomplishment, the formal structure of the organization, the informal structure of the organization, the people who work in the organization, and the people who deal with the organization. He or she must find strategies for managing those areas of impact. The impact on task accomplishment may be minor or major. A leader needs to spend time defining how things are going to be accomplished to make sure that no task is left undone. A focus on the future scenario by the leader helps to ensure that results will continue to be attained at the appropriate level.

Often, an organizational change involves a restructuring of the organization. This may be done to speed things up, address customer issues better, or improve relationships among work units. Even if a change is not expected to lead to a restructuring, it is important for the leader to consider the possibility that this might happen and what should be done if it does. This is equally true of the organization's informal structure.

It is known that about 30 percent of people like change. They tend to be easy to lead through change. The other 70 percent do not like change. A leader must make sure that the organization's change agents have approaches for dealing with those people who don't like change, as they are more likely to be the ones that will resist it. People will resist change to different degrees, so change agents need more than one approach. People outside the organization who will feel the impact of a change must be taken into account in these approaches. These people tend to be vendors, customers, regulators, competitors, and other stakeholders.

The budget for the change is a major consideration for the leader. Money has to be allocated for out-of-the-ordinary expenditures caused by the change. The budget plan must be monitored, and the leader must hold people accountable for executing it. Variances should be addressed immediately in order to avoid spiraling costs. The leader should get explanations when more money is asked for.

Once the changes are committed to, the leader should assess how ready the organization is for it. Are the employees ready? Do people have the needed skills? These may include change-management skills and necessary horizontal or vertical skill enhancement. It is extremely important that the leader have information about skill requirements during the change and upon full implementation of the change. An up-to-date skills cataloguing tool for all employees would be helpful. Sometimes employees are completely ready for a change; a minor or major crisis may have employees looking to the organization's leadership for relief. Sometimes people are ready because they see a major opportunity in the marketplace. Knowledge about the readiness of people is essential because it indicates how easy or difficult implementation of the change might be. The leader may decide to postpone the change or to move more slowly in order to ensure a smooth transition.

Timing of needed training is crucial for change success. It must be addressed with particularly precise analysis.

Any possible changes in job responsibilities should be accounted for. How will people be prepared to handle added or different responsibilities? How will tasks be shared? Will people be required to work overtime? How tight will deadlines be? What tasks will the leader have to monitor more closely than usual? The leader must make sure that there are no surprises. If there are going to be shifts from one person to another, a specific plan for the changeover must be in place. Any extension in work hours needs to be discussed ahead of time, as should issues around deadlines, given that changes could cause workload imbalances.

What policies and procedures will be changed? How will the new ones be explained and reinforced?

Regardless of a leader's style, periods of change can test the leader's flexibility. The leader must be willing to more tightly or more loosely keep an eye on things. Which things is a matter of the leader's main focus points.

The leader will want to be aware of how people respond, as well as how successful the implementation of new policies, procedures, or products are. During a period of change, organizational goals, departmental goals, work-unit goals, and personal goals may conflict. How will leaders encourage people to work with other departments? Will they be asked to be more flexible or more patient? Who will handle any problems that arise and how will they be handled? Conflicts must be anticipated and addressed with effective conflict-management strategies.

Change also has effects outside the organization. Are the organization's customers, vendors and suppliers, and others ready for the impact of the change? All of these are things that the leader must take into account and plan for. Ongoing vigilance is required.

Finally, the efforts to ensure success often are more than a leader can handle alone. It is important to have the support and effective participation of other executives and members of upper management during organizational change. So the leader must ensure that these persons are well prepared to lead change in general and to implement the specific change in particular.

Evaluation

Change doesn't necessarily occur as planned. It can be rough and tumble. As I said above, the leader needs to monitor how well the change is being integrated. This will allow him or her to take action if required and to reinforce positive integration of the change.

Along with his or her change-management experts (key change agents), the leader must develop an approach for evaluating the progress of the change, including a list of special criteria for evaluation.

There are some considerations that must be made during a change project regardless of what the change target is. The following list can be used by the leader to identify the particular aspects that he or she needs people to focus on.

1. Productivity: Will productivity go up or down? If it goes down, for how long and how far can we let it go down? This will require more-careful-than-usual monitoring of the productivity-measurement system that is already in place. The leader must make sure that there is a certain bottom point below which productivity is not allowed to fall.

2. Job satisfaction: Job satisfaction is a major issue for many people during and after organizational change, and it is likely to dip during the change. Leaders must find ways to crank it up again. The best way to create such energy is by asking employees what will be required to increase job satisfaction and then taking actions accordingly. Either an employee survey or a focus group can be used regularly to keep up with this information.

3. Profits: Change projects should be evaluated in terms of their impact on profits. It may be reasonable to assume that a planned change will lead to higher profits, but the financial picture should be monitored very carefully to determine whether or not the change is of value. Any slowdown in profits must be analyzed.

4. Resources: What resources and how much of them will be available during the change? Resource availability must be consistent with what people need to get through the change. Resources should not be less available than what people have become used to.

5. Stress: Change can be stressful. A little stress is fine and can be energizing; however, if a change causes too much stress, it can lead to too much tension in the system. Leaders must monitor the stress level and find a way to neutralize it if it becomes too great.

6. Quality of work: Leaders need to monitor the quality of work during the period of change. Quality of output can go up or down with or without change, but during a change, people may begin to focus on some wrong task issues. If these have a negative impact on the quality of work, the organization suffers. Leaders must be quick to respond to any downfall in the quality of work. It is equally important to recognize people whose work exceeds the norm.

7. Communication: One of the keys to successful implementation of change is good communication. The leader must make sure that there is accurate communication about the change. This may be by means of frequent departmental meetings, an electronic newsletter, video- or teleconferences, etc. Meetings must be more open than usual to discussion and clarification. During a period of change, *precision* in communication is very important. Rumors must be kept in control. More than ever, people

need to know exactly what is going on. Listening is essential to good communication. During change, it is even more important. Leaders must listen to people who just want to blow off steam and to people who have suggestions on how to better manage the change. Leaders should also seek out and listen to people who may have useful things to say.

Personal Assessment of Leading for Change

Questions for Reflection

1. How do you normally respond to change?

2. What are the best ways for you to be supportive of change efforts?

3. How should you work with (a) people who resist change and (b) people who embrace change?

4. Next time you are involved a change effort, what actions will you take to enhance the results of the change effort?

Personal Actions

1. Description of what you did:

2. Were any resources required?

3. How were you able to sustain the effort?

4. Description of how people reacted:

5. How creative were you?

6. Quantitative assessment of what you did: What was the impact?

7. How did you know what the impact was?

8. Ways and places to spread this best practice:

9. What is the possible long-term impact?

10. What's the payback to you?

Chapter 6

Foster Conflict Management

The worst conflict I was involved in as a child was with one of my best friends. Other friends egged us on, and we agreed to have it out after school. To this day, I'm convinced that I "won" the fight but what I mostly remember from the incident is that you can get very tense and irrational during a conflict and waste your energy. I remember bad feelings lingering. Eventually, through the intercession of our mothers, my friend and I made up, but the destructive aspects of the conflict got me thinking. I had learned that it was preferable to address conflict productively. When you sweep it under the rug, the negativity accumulates and is de-energizing. When you fight, nothing is really resolved. In short, unhealthy ways of dealing with conflict are destructive.

As I grew professionally, it became clear to me that what I had experienced that day had impacted me significantly. Although some conflict is inevitable, you have to deal with it.

There can positive outcomes from conflict. Dealing properly with conflict brings people closer together and is energizing.

Conflict in the Workplace

There are many potential conflict situations in a work environment. Knowing how they arise and how to manage them are critical skills for leaders.

Sources of Conflict

Conflict can come from many possible sources. Everyone has been in a situation in which there was disagreement about how to complete a project by a certain date. The disagreement may have centered on the nature of the project or some particular stage of it, on the deadline, or on those involved (the number of people involved, the particular individuals, their skill levels, their interactions, and so on). Often, there is lack of clarity about what the actual disagreement is. It is always important to know what the source of a conflict is. In general, there are seven possible sources:

1. The first potential source of conflict is what people think is important, what they value. Even when we work hard to create value congruence in organizations, there will still be times when people's different perceptions about what is important are the source of conflict. These perceptions can be about interpersonal issues, such as working as a team player or loyalty to a boss. They can be about values that people have about the work itself—about a particular task, regulation, procedure, schedule, or outcome.

68

2. The second possible source of conflict is about how the organization is put together. Conflicts often are about what department someone is in or where someone is located on the organizational chart.

3. The third source is about information (e.g., access to the information, what the information means, and what action should be taken as a result of that information).

4. Another source of conflict has to do with resources: personnel, finances, the physical plant, and technology. Almost every leader, manager, department head, and so on, believes that he or she needs more resources. So there tends to be disagreement about who has what and who gets what.

5. Conflict also arises over standards and procedures. Even when there are procedural manuals, someone may think that he or she has found a better way. In the absence of an established procedure, people "wing it" to get things done. Obviously, there is a lot of room for disagreement about how things "should" be done.

6. Different perspectives about goals and objectives are a source of conflict. What are we trying to accomplish today, this week, this month, or this year? Such conflict can be difficult to overcome. This is why attaining values congruence and linking strategic elements are essential survival strategies for an organization.

7. Expectations are another source of conflict. People may not understand what their expectations are in an organization. Others may not be satisfied with their expectations (including their job tasks, their sources of communication, and their influence over

their work). Some people report to more than one person. Sometimes an organization is in a state of transition. All these situations can cause conflict.

Once we know what the possible sources of conflict are and we see a situation where there is conflict, we can identify what the source of it is. This is important because we don't want to attempt to deal with a conflict inappropriately. We want to resolve the conflict that actually exists.

Stages of Conflict

Conflict normally proceeds through four stages. These are:
1. Anticipation: In this stage we may feel that there is going to be some dispute or knocking of heads together.
2. Consciousness of Differences: As the conversation continues, we become aware that there is a true difference and of what that difference is.
3. Picking Sides: In this stage, we decide what we are for and what we are against.
4. Open Hostility: The conflict escalates into a dysfunctional state, and some form of open hostility breaks out.

Typical Responses to Conflict

Studies conducted by the U.S. Army indicated that people generally have one or two immediate responses to conflict, no matter what their level in the hierarchy. One is called the flight response: moving away from the conflict physically and emotionally, through verbal and/or nonverbal communication, as fast as one can. The second response is the fight response; it is an aggressive, pound-them-down-and-win-at-all-costs approach. Interestingly, the subjects in the Army studies were all men. Later research revealed that some women have another approach: they talk out the issues with other women. But then they still have to decide how to deal with the conflict. The important thing to remember is that the two primary responses are extreme and usually are counterproductive. A response somewhere in between the extremes is more productive and will lead to a more positive outcome.

Managing Conflict

A workplace conflict must be addressed and resolved as soon as possible. If it is not, the situation is likely to become disruptive if not destructive. When conflict is allowed to continue, it causes stress. People take sides. They become upset and they do and say things that they may not normally do. People who are under a lot of stress also make more mistakes and have more health problems. Relationships are harmed, and work is derailed. Therefore, the elimination (or at least the control of) conflict in the workplace is very important.

When conflict is dealt with appropriately—that is, constructively—relationships improve; new perspectives are considered; both sides win; and people recognize that their visions, missions, and goals have a lot more in common than they previously realized.

The first thing a leader needs to do in a conflict situation is to quickly frame the situation for himself or herself. This means developing a perspective from which all conflicts are managed. This perspective includes many different aspects.

1. It is important to protect the dignity of every person involved in the conflict. This helps them to maintain the perspective they need to negotiate or otherwise deal with the conflict and helps to avoid hard feelings and other repercussions afterward. As part of this, it is important to insist that each person show respect for the other persons and for their situations and perspectives.

2. It is essential to listen attentively and to insist that the opposing parties actually listen to each other. This is of critical importance in a conflict situation. Helping other people to listen to and focus on the needs and perspectives of the opposing party often produces an in-kind response that leads to the meeting of both sides' needs.

3. The leader must help the parties to identify what the focus of the conflict should be on: the big picture or what is best for the organization, the department, or the majority of the people involved.

4. The leader should help the conflicting parties to look for mutuality. This means identifying what they have in common. This is a great starting point and increases the probability of a quick resolution.

5. Finally, the leader should point out that there's usually more than one way to do something. This means adopting a will-

ingness to accept multiple perspectives. Even many grown-ups need to learn that if you get the result you're after, doing something in a way that is different from the one you had envisioned is okay. This realization alone can reduce many conflicts.

One of the most important things to do when it comes to conflict is to determine what approach each individual is taking to dealing with the conflict. Some typical approaches are: 1) letting it slide and hoping it will go away, 2) just wanting to get along and live together peacefully (which may result in giving in before the conflict is actually resolved), 3) making trades, 4) remaining upbeat about the situation and the people involved in it and continuing to work for resolution, 5) taking charge and taking over, and 6) refusing to negotiate and threatening (e.g., to go to a higher authority or to sue).

Another important element is how each party—and even a third-party consultant who is helping to deal with the situation—will define "success" in resolving the conflict. The leader needs to know what measures of success are considered appropriate by the people involved. These serve as indicators of how to proceed.

The criteria for success must be developed before either or both of the parties are able to feel comfortable with the outcome. For example, each party in the conflict may want a certain level of resources if the conflict is about resources. Success is defined as gaining the level of resources deemed necessary. If the level of resources gained is below the amount deemed required for success, the conflict is viewed as not successfully resolved.

The leader must make it clear that constructive conflict resolution occurs when people work hard at doing the following:

1. Listening carefully.
2. Stating what they think the other party's situation is.
3. Offering something that the other party wants or needs.
4. Keeping in mind that there is something that they would like to gain from the resolution of the conflict.
5. Keeping in mind that new ideas may help to solve the conflict.
6. Working to generate new viewpoints, ideas, and options.
7. Acknowledging that the conflict is an opportunity to improve the situation or build a relationship.
8. Looking for the bigger picture (e.g., how deadlines can be met, how better business results can be obtained).
9. Acknowledging that they have more in common with the other party than may have first been apparent.
10. Offering to resume the discussion after a cooling-off period, during which both parties have time to think more about what they want to say.
11. Resuming the discussion and working through the conflict.
12. Coming to an agreement, with each party stating verbally (and perhaps in writing) what they think the resolution is.
13. Working to implement the agreement.

Quick Conflict Resolution

Often a leader doesn't have a great deal of time to devote to resolving a conflict and may need to end it quickly. In such a case, he or she may ask for specific, up-front preparation from the parties involved. This means requiring the following behaviors:

1. Working to implement the agreement.
2. Being assertive rather than manipulative, aggressive, or passive.
3. Presenting just the facts.
4. Providing specific examples, not generalizations.
5. Knowing exactly what you want and what you might settle for.
6. Knowing exactly what the other party wants.
7. Making exchanges or trade offs.
8. Agreeing on a solution.
9. If appropriate, developing a plan and setting a schedule for implementing the solution.

The difference between quick conflict resolution and normal conflict resolution is that there is a great deal of knowledge going into the former about what is wanted, what can be gained, what can be lost, what can be traded, and what the other side wants. Normal conflict resolution takes more time because there is not as much specific preparation and information required up front.

Using a Third Party

Sometimes, leaders have to call for third-party intervention in a conflict. This may involve hiring a conflict-resolution specialist, such as a consultant or a mediator. In some cases, the leader has to adopt one of these roles. (This assumes that the leader is comfortable in assuming the role.) Third-party consultants and mediators often are more objective in trying to solve problems. They listen carefully for feelings and interpretations and feed them back to the disputing parties. They usually are more flexible and creative than the disputing parties and they often make specific suggestions about options to be considered or the need for one of the parties to make a change.

The role of the consultant or mediator often is not to strike a balance between the needs of the disputants but to achieve an outcome that is best for the organization. Obviously, the consultant or mediator is likely to have a more objective perspective on that than either of the disputing parties. Even if the third party is the manager of the disputing parties, this is likely to be true.

Another type of third-party intervener, the arbitrator, often has the right to make a final decision if the disputing parties cannot reach agreement.

Improving One's Conflict-Management Skills

Leaders who want to be better at managing conflict can improve their skills. They can read about conflict management and practice it.

They can attend leadership-education programs on conflict management.

Part of learning is assessing information and how to apply it. A leader who wants to improve his or her conflict-management skills can try the following exercise. Divide a piece of paper in half vertically. On the left side, make a list of the behaviors that you think will lead to managing disagreements and managing conflict constructively. On the right side, list the behaviors that you think only aggravate conflict situations. Imagine yourself in a conflict situation with a peer or boss or direct report exhibiting the behaviors that lead to effective conflict management. Then make note of what is on the other side of the page and plan what you will do to avoid those behaviors in the future.

Not All Conflict Must Be Resolved by the Leader

It is important to know that not all conflicts need to be dealt with. Some conflicts must be dealt with; some could be dealt with; and some can be ignored. The only way to know how to treat a specific conflict is to analyze the situation. You can ask the following twelve questions. By the time you get to the last question, you should have an answer. The questions are:

1. What is the conflict about?
2. Who is in conflict?
3. What is the nature of the relationship between the people involved?
4. What are people feeling about the conflict?

5. What do the conflicting parties want?

6. Are there any underlying issues?

7. How are business results being affected?

8. What would happen if nothing were done?

9. How much time and energy would be required to resolve the conflict?

10. Is it worth the time and energy required to resolve the conflict?

11. How will the organization be stronger if this conflict is re-solved?

12. Can this conflict be resolved quickly by some action that I can take?

Personal Assessment of Conflict Management

Questions for Reflection

1. How much conflict in your organization is bought into the open and discussed?

2. How well is conflict resolved in your organization?

3. In your organization, how skilled are individuals at resolving conflict?

4. What do you think needs to be done to reduce important conflicts in your organization?

5. What needs to be done to better manage conflict in your organization?

Personal Actions

1. Description of what you did:

2. How were you able to sustain the effort?

3. How did people react?

4. What about the people who didn't react?

5. How creative were you?

6. Quantitative assessment of what you did: What was the impact?

7. How did you know what the impact was?

8. What is the possible long-term impact?

9. What's the payback to you?

Chapter 7

Develop a Performance-Management System

One of the jobs that I had as a teenager was working in a fast-food restaurant. Soon after being hired, I had to work on a Friday night, which was the busiest time of the week. I was working as a sandwich assembler in position number two. There was another sandwich assembler in position number one. Normally, the assembler in position one had to respond most quickly to what the customer ordered. About one-fourth of the way into the evening, the restaurant manager told the other sandwich assembler and me to switch places. The other assembler became upset and asked the manager why the change had been made, as he had been working there much longer than I had. The manager explained that I was faster, so I would take position number one. The other assembler was not happy with this explanation. This was one of my earliest experiences with performance management, as well as, process improvement. The manager realized that there was a way to increase the speed at which orders could be filled as part of an effort to manage the performance of the restaurant during peak hours.

Reasons for Performance-Management Systems

1. Leaders have the responsibility to ensure that the organization and its departments and functions perform as well as they possibly can. High levels of performance can contribute significantly to the bottom line. There are formal and informal performance-management systems. Although specific, formal, performance-management systems occasionally come under fire from researchers, consultants, and executives, there still is a need for some kind of approach to managing the performance of individuals and the overall enterprise. Leaders engage in performance-management programs because they want to improve productivity. Productivity improves when people get continual feedback about how they are doing, whether they are on track or not, and how obstacles can be removed. Then they can make appropriate improvements so that they can be more productive.

2. A performance-management system helps to identify learning needs for individuals so that they can be sent to training and development programs.

3. Performance management gives people an opportunity to grow professionally. As their performance improves and as they receive more training to develop themselves, there is a payoff to the organization.

4. When performance management is in place, formally or informally, leaders and followers communicate more. This is certainly to be valued.

5. When a performance-management system is fully operative, its different components—such as assigning responsibility, monitoring progress, and coaching the progress—provide an opportunity for individual employees' goals and the organization's goals to be aligned. Alignment of personal and organizational goals is highly motivational.

6. Performance management also makes it easier to administer a compensation plan. A performance-management system provides data for promotional decisions or for moving people.

7. A performance-management system provides a record of employee performance. This is important for legal reasons. It is easier for an organization to defend itself when it has the facts that a performance-management system includes in its database.

8. The bottom line is that the CEO must spotlight the manager's performance management role as important enough to focus time and attention on dealing with others in respectful ways.

Essentials of Performance-Management Systems

The most important thing to remember about a performance-management system is that it needs to be anchored to some of the things we know about human behavior. We have known for a long time that people will work toward the goal that they are expected to and will try to use the behaviors that they are expected to in order to complete a task. People are more productive when they know what they are required to do. So the first thing to keep in mind is that performance management must understand and establish expectations.

For decades, organizational theorists, researchers, consultants, and executives have been trying to get people to participate in decisions that affect them at work. Performance management is one of a leader's responsibilities in which participation is very important. People who have a say in their performance, based on a realistic understanding of what involvement means, normally perform well.

The next important concept is measurement. People like to know how well they are doing. They also want to know how they are being measured. People seem to perform better when they know what the target is, how the path to hitting the target has been determined, and how accomplishment toward the goal will be measured.

Communication is the last essential issue in performance management. The leader needs to communicate where people stand and how their performance is perceived. This is true no matter what level the leader is on in the organizational chart. The need to communicate on an ongoing basis and in an understandable manner is essential. Furthermore, effective performance management requires two-way communication, rather than just top-down communication.

Establishing a Performance-Management Program

Performance management is part of a three-pronged leadership effort. The first aspect is performance planning. This involves identifying (given the amount of resources that an organization has) how it can be expected to achieve it goals and objectives, financial and otherwise. The second aspect is standards of performance or expectations—the goals and objectives that people are expected to obtain. This involves gaining agreement between the leader and followers as well as identifying opportunities to change and improve performance. The third aspect is performance assessment, the effort of managing job accomplishment and coaching for improvement so that performance is more aligned with achieving the best possible results.

Performance management is not the same as performance appraisal or performance evaluation. It is not merely checking off a bunch of boxes and sending them to the human resources department. It is an ongoing, integrated system.

Establishing Performance Expectations

Using their knowledge of the organization and its processes, leaders need to identify each job by title, write a job description (including lists of tasks, amount of tasks, possible timing for each task, and other responsibilities and obligations) and define the expectations for that job. This means a list of results that are expected, including output, timing, and so on. At every level of the organization, it is important to identify as specifically as possible what is to be accomplished. These performance factors are what the organization will use to measure the performance of individuals, departments, and other work units. A human resources department or a human resources consultant can provide invaluable assistance to a leader in this regard.

Performance factors also might include such things as communicating, working well with others, being responsive to change, planning, organizing, and showing initiative. These are only examples; there are many factors that organizations use in assessing performance. Leaders at all levels of the organization need to define the factors using a cascading effect (cascading down and perhaps across organizational functions).

Identifying and Allocating Resources

Next, the resources that are *needed* to complete each job task and achieve the desired objectives must be identified. Resources include the physical plant, time, financial support, technology, and personnel. The resources that are *available* must be identified and allocated and, if there is a gap between what is available and what is needed, plans must be made to fill that gap. It is also important to make sure that employees know that they will have the resources they need to meet their job expectations.

Communicating Performance Expectations

The third thing to do is to meet with employees and talk about job expectations. Identifying job expectations is a critical step. This may involve give and take in terms of influence. To establish performance expectations, the supervisor needs to sit down with each employee and discuss his or her specific tasks and the amount and timing of each one, any other job responsibilities, the outcomes that are expected, and how these will be measured. The supervisor also should offer assistance to the employee whenever it is needed.

The importance of this step cannot be overemphasized. Determining what performance is required should never involve mind reading. There should always be a precise road map for knowing what the accountabilities are for every employee. This allows them to direct their energies and resources to the requirements of their jobs. It has long been said that the only way you can attempt to hit a target is if you can see it.

Establishing a Monitoring System

Each employee needs to know how he or she is going to be monitored and how his or her work is going to be assessed. The most important consideration here is how to evaluate how well the work is done. Leaders must determine how often they will measure performance accomplishment, whether it be daily, weekly, monthly, or quarterly.

Delivering Feedback

The fifth step is making sure that leaders have feedback systems in place and that feedback actually is provided. Feedback systems include consideration of how feedback will be delivered, how often it will be done, where it will be done, and what systems will be used to track it.

It is very difficult for some people to master the art of giving effective feedback. Some people naturally soft-pedal everything they say about another person. Others come across as being too harsh or too judgmental. Leaders and managers need to be aware if they have a tendency to be too lenient, too optimistic, too severe or critical, or too negative. Most leaders and managers would benefit from specific training in delivering feedback. Entire books have been written about the various forms of feedback (critical, constructive, and reinforcing) and when it is appropriate to use them. The different types of feedback all are useful and should be used as needed in performance-management systems. In general, leaders and managers need to understand how important it is to provide positive feedback and encouragement. Applied research suggests that an environment in which there is an emphasis on positive feedback is a more successful environment. Leaders should set examples for everyone in the organization by providing appropriate positive feedback.

It is very easy for individuals who are receiving feedback about their performance to react negatively. This is especially true if the individuals feel that the feedback is a one-directional conversation. It should always be a two-way conversation.

Unfortunately, some performance will need to be assessed as lacking. The creation of a culture of open communication in the organization will help to keep the delivery of negative feedback from being too uncomfortable. However, without trust and openness, it can be very difficult. A leader who is trying to create a culture of performance management should make sure that everyone is trained in how to engage others in difficult conversations about performance. There are six important things to keep in mind when providing negative feedback:

1. Make sure that it is done privately.

2. Be very descriptive and be sure to include the impact that the performance is having on the organization.

3. Encourage the employee to talk about his or her view of the problem and to suggest how things might be improved.

4. Reach agreement on what needs to be done, how it will be done, when it is going to be done, and the role that the leader or manager will play in helping the employee to improve his or her performance.

5. Make sure that there is complete understanding of how the employee's performance will be monitored and any consequences, positive or negative, that will result from the monitoring activity.

6. Establish a trail of documentation whenever there is an issue of poor performance. Extraordinary performance should also be documented, but it is more important that poor performance be documented because the outcome may have to be defended legally.

Developing Employees

One of the important aspects of performance management is the identification of development needs. Leaders need to build an organizational culture for performance management that emphasizes growth and development as opposed to punishment and firing. Using the performance-management system to identify needs for development can be one of the more positive opportunities for a leader. Employee development should proceed along certain lines. First, conversations with employees about their performance often reveal a need to strengthen or improve somebody's knowledge or skills. This is the beginning of a development effort for that employee. It is important that the employee be open to development. Some people want to grow in knowledge and skill while others are happy to stay as they are. The leader or manager must be specific about what the development opportunity is and help the employee to recognize that there are options for gaining improved knowledge or skills. This could include in-house training programs, cross-training, outside education, and a new job assignment, among other things. Lastly, of course, the leader and follower need to agree on what kind of development plan is going to be put into place. Time lines should be established for certain activities.

Conclusion

A leader who develops a formal or informal performance-management system makes the statement that the organization believes in developing its human resources. This requires an ongoing effort and a great deal of clarity about expectations, objectives, monitoring approaches, feedback, and employee development. In an effective performance-management system, everyone knows what the leaders and managers expect from one another and their subordinates. When people know what is expected of them, they become more self-motivated, accept personal accountability better, and work better with others. Effective performance management eliminates the surprises in expectations and assessment that can be demotivating. With an effective performance-management system, it is possible to gain greater commitment and productivity from employees so that the organization achieves the desired results. The leader who builds and reinforces a culture of performance management also makes a statement about the value of productivity, quality, and added value because everyone in the organization is engaged in performance management. The positive outcomes affect the leaders, the employees, and all stakeholders.

Personal Assessment of Performance Management

Questions for Reflection

1. What are the driving forces behind your organization's performance-management system?

2. How much feedback do employees give about the performance-management system's processes?

3. How would you rate the success of the performance-management process in your organization?

4. How would you rate the performance-appraisal process in your organization?

5. What improvements would you make to the existing systems?

Personal Actions

1. Description of what you did:

2. Were any resources required?

3. How were you able to sustain the effort?

4. Description of how people reacted:

5. How creative were you?

6. Quantitative assessment of what you did: What was the impact?

7. How did you know what the impact was?

8. What is the possible long-term impact?

9. What's the payback to you?

10. What's the status now? Are things still progressing?

Chapter 8

Coach for Results

I was twelve years old the first time I received real coaching. My parents had decided to let me play football on a neighborhood team. We traveled to other neighborhoods to play other teams. My coach was Mr. Lamneck. He had two sons who played on the team. I thought it must be hard for Mr. Lamneck to coach a team on which his sons played and still be fair about everything. He was, though.

Mr. Lamneck was very precise about what he wanted us to be able to do. He took time with each individual and conveyed his expectations so that the boy could perform well individually and as part of a team. He was good at getting us excited about our "performance."

Coaching is about getting people to perform well. Coaching is about getting people excited about what they are doing. That is what Mr. Lamneck did so very well. Leaders must do the same.

The Leader As a Coach

Leaders have a responsibility to coach, because not all performance is what it needs to be. Expectations are not always met. Occasionally individual success is made a priority, while behaviors that would make the total organization a success are ignored. A leader needs to engage in coaching because it is important to help a valued employee improve his or her performance by using encouragement and transferring knowledge. A leader may not be able to coach every employee directly, but he or she has a responsibility to establish a coaching approach with his or her direct reports and also to create a coaching culture so that people can successfully improve their performance. This will allow the organization to gain from what it has already invested in its people.

Characteristics and Skills of Effective Coaches

There are certain characteristics and skills that a leader must have or develop in order to be a successful coach; these are part of the leader's overall professional repertoire. They are as follows:

1. The coach is articulate; he or she is able to speak and write well in order to deliver messages that convey with precision the expectations that the organization has for the employee's performance. Being articulate includes being as detailed as possible so that the person understands exactly what is expected.

2. The coach is respectful. He or she understands that employees do not all perform at the same level. This is true even if all have received the same training and have the same experience. So a good coach respects whatever the best level of performance is that an individual is able to obtain. There are so many variables that affect performance that one cannot even assume that one individual is going to perform at the same level all the time.

This does not mean, however, that nothing should be done about substandard performance. If an employee isn't performing well, something must be done.

3. The coach is direct. He or she avoids beating around the bush and explains exactly what the expectation is, exactly where the performance deficit is, and the gap that needs to be closed in order for the performance to be acceptable. The coach communicates in terms that the employee understands, which is the other aspect of being direct.

4. The coach is humble, realizing that he or she never performs perfectly all the time, especially when new at a job. People develop knowledge and skills over time before they become valued assets of the organization. The best leaders and coaches remember where they have been and they appreciate everyone's efforts. They do not brag about their own achievements.

5. The coach is task oriented. He or she knows what it takes to get the job done and produce results—what tasks are required and what behaviors are required. Although the coach pays attention to the relationship he or she has with each employee, he or she also needs to be certain that the specifics of the task are carried out for the good of the whole organization. The coach needs to know what technologies, job aids, and other people can facilitate the successful accomplishment of the task.

6. An effective coach pays attention to detail.

7. An effective coach is good at analyzing opportunities and situations.

8. An effective coach is good at observing behavior, which can be difficult to achieve. Several people can see the same thing and interpret it differently. Leaders who will serve as coaches must work to develop the skill of accurate behavioral observation.

9. A good coach is concerned about the efficient use of resources, whether they be human resources, financial resources, or technological resources. The coach expects the employee to get everything he or she can out of the available resources.

10. A good coach is flexible and is willing to take risks from time to time. This may include giving an employee some room for "different" performance on occasion if the situation allows for it.

11. A good coach knows how to ask effective questions. He or she also knows when to ask open-ended questions and when to ask closed questions.

12. A good coach knows how to provide timely, specific, and helpful feedback. This skill is even more important in coaching than it is in managing or leading, so the leader who needs to be a coach must learn to give effective feedback.

13. A good coach sees the coaching role as a teaching *and* learning process. The person being coached is the primary learner, but because it is an interactive process, the coach and the employee are learning from each other. A good coach takes personal responsibility for the employee's behavior. The coach sees his or her responsibility in helping the person to grow and become

successful. Poor coaches—and poor leaders, for that matter—try to blame others for negative outcomes.

14. A good coach uses supportive communication, focuses on the future, and is able to relate to all kinds of personalities.

15. An effective coach is positive and optimistic (or appears to be). This is a very important aspect of the coaching process. Mr. Lamneck was always positive and upbeat; he always motivated us by drawing us to where he wanted us to be. The year that he was my coach, I also played baseball on another neighborhood team. The baseball coach was not so positive and optimistic; in fact, he was negative and beat people down. I did not grow in athletic skill under that coach.

Whenever a leader needs to be a coach, he or she must make the time for it. In order to make it go well, the leader also must be very clear about the purpose of the coaching. It may be to help a person grow into a new position, to help a person grow in knowledge or skill, or to help the person become eligible for promotion. Being clear about the purpose of the coaching will help the leader to select the right coaching interventions.

Coaching takes preparation and practice. I have been coaching in some form for about thirty-five years. Whenever I know that I have to coach someone, I think about it and write things down. I also practice what I am going to do, with the help of a tape recorder or video camera. Preparation and practice increase the chances of having a positive experience and a successful outcome.

Elements of an Effective Coaching Relationship

In addition to the qualities of the coach, there are other elements of an effective coaching relationship. Part of coaching someone is that the communication about performance is ongoing. Coaching entails follow-up and reinforcement, and these require continual communication. Coaching is not a one-time event.

The steps in the coaching process are pretty straightforward. First, the coach must set up the meeting with the person to be coached for a mutually convenient time and place.

At the beginning of the first session, the coach and the employee must identify (and agree on) the exact nature of the problem. This can be achieved by the coach's asking questions that lead the employee to answers about what the problem might be. Some leaders would prefer to simply tell the employee what the problem is. The problem with this approach is there may not be agreement. If agreement by the employee is missing, he or she probably will not be committed to the process or to a successful outcome.

Next, the coach should ask the employee what the appropriate solution(s) might be. If the employee does not offer an answer, the coach should offer a solution and ask the employee if he or she has any thoughts about it. If the employee does not respond or does not like the solution, the coach should continue to offer solutions and ask the employee if he or she now has anything to suggest.

The next step is for the coach and employee to rationally examine all the possible solutions and to agree on a particular solution. This might involve using a discussion matrix or consequence analysis. Then they develop and agree on a plan of action to implement the chosen solution. A plan of action usually includes "who" will do "what" by "when." It rarely includes the "how." It includes specifics, time lines, and how the success of the employee will be measured and evaluated.

The succeeding step is the development of a plan for follow-up as implementation occurs. This follow-up could be daily, weekly, or monthly. It depends on the substance of the coaching issue. The simpler the issue, the faster it should be resolved. This would probably mean follow-up as often as once a day or once a week. If the issue is a larger one with a longer time cycle (that is, the task has a longer time cycle than the plan for follow-up) it can be discussed every couple of weeks. Of course, follow-up by electronic means may be part of this plan.

Each step in the coaching process should be reinforced. The leader-coach should praise success. This makes the employee feel that he or she is headed in the right direction and increases his or her commitment to continue working on the improvement.

The last step is to coach more if it is needed. One round of coaching doesn't always work perfectly, but the coaching process does work. From time to time, it may simply need to be repeated. The coach must determine how much more coaching is needed before deciding to take different steps with the employee.

While all of this is going on, the coach must listen with empathy, maintain eye contact, avoid interrupting, reinforce the employee's participation (for example, by nodding or making positive comments), paraphrase as appropriate to show understanding, and repeat important information to make sure the employee understands it.

The leader who is being a coach has a unique opportunity to become directly involved and to help people develop. This is an essential task of a good leader: helping people to perform better, especially the leader's direct reports. It is also a very rewarding experience.

Personal Assessment of Coaching

Questions for Reflection

1. How good are your coaching skills?

2. How pervasive is coaching in your organization?

3. To what extent does coaching in your organization have an impact on people's performance?

4. What do leaders focus on in generating more successful coaching?

Personal Actions

1. Description of what you did in a coaching session:

2. How were you able to sustain the effort?

3. Description of how the person being coached reacted:

4. How creative were you?

5. Quantitative assessment of what you did: What was the impact?

6. How did you know what the impact was?

7. Ways to spread this best practice:

8. What is the possible long-term impact?

9. What's the payback to you?

Chapter 9

Create a Business-Process Improvement Orientation

A s a teenager I would order pizza, then go to pick it up. I watched the employees use a huge spatula to manipulate the pizza in a large, hot oven. Some years later I noticed a new way of cooking pizza: each pizza was put in a pan, the ingredients were put on in layers, and the whole thing was put on a chain and passed through a cooking tunnel and came out cooked. The obvious improvement was that somebody didn't have to open the oven door, turn the pizza, and then go through that cycle again a few minutes later. Someone had invented a new process for cooking pizza.

Business processes can become static and inflexible. However, if you examine them, it often is possible to find a better way to do something. It's part of a leader's job to find better ways to do things. Sometimes this involves changing a technology; sometimes it involves changing a procedure. For example, as a young director of human resources, I found that getting approval to fill a job vacancy was quite cumbersome; it took five signatures. Applications sat on people's desks, and they didn't get around to signing them, so positions would be open for a long time and the line managers would be screaming because productivity fell. I streamlined the process, although, in those days, we didn't call it business-process improvement. I got the number of signatures down to two, and both had alternatives, so if somebody wasn't available there was a backup person to sign.

Business-Process Improvement Is About Adding Value

Leaders should continually take actions to make sure they add value to the customer/client experience. There are lots of ways to do this. Business-process improvement is an important example because it can lead to better use of resources, more satisfied customers, and greater job satisfaction for employees.

It begins by having the attitude that all business processes can be improved. Once that kind of thinking is accepted, you can begin to improve the current processes. You can find ways to simplify things and ways to speed things up. Often, but not always, this includes changing a technology. There are other things that also help a great deal, including planning how to use resources.

Establishing a Process-Improvement Culture

Leaders have an opportunity to improve business processes by establishing an organizational culture that accepts and knows how to execute business-process improvement. Everyone has to know it's important, that it impacts the customers, employees, costs, and productivity. Second, they have to have the skills. In some organizations, the skills are in the industrial engineering department, the process-improvement department, or something similar. However, individual employees are always involved. If employees are empowered to improve business processes, they make changes that are longer lasting and that they are committed to.

One of the more important aspects of training for employees is teaching them how to create process flow diagrams. A process flow diagram is a tool that is used to map out each of the steps in a business process or procedure. This allows an employee, group of employees, or supervisor to visually identify how a task is performed. Review of the steps is carried out to determine if there are steps that could be combined or eliminated. The use of such a diagram usually leads to an improvement in productivity.

Creating a culture that is supportive of business-process improvement is done through education, by reinforcing successful efforts, by publicizing successful efforts, and by making sure that the reward system rewards such efforts. It also means that the knowledge that employees have is put to use to improve what they do; that begins with the leader using his or her knowledge base to improve what he or she does. The effort must be organization wide, with all members of the organization engaged in using their knowledge to improve processes. Employees will seek improvements because they don't want problems to recur. Like the organization's leaders, the employees want the best value-adding processes in place.

The key to success in establishing such a culture is leadership. The process is built on a foundation of leadership commitment and involvement.

Initiating Process Improvement

The first step is to identify and choose a process to be reviewed. This normally is done by a group of employees who are consistently involved in the process. They usually respond to a problem, complaint, or the discovery of a best practice that could be imported.

Analyzing the process is the next step. First, a process flow diagram is developed. This usually involves the group of employees referred to above. The group reviews the diagram and identifies any slowdowns, gaps, and other problems that can be eliminated. The group then decides which ones they will invest their time and energy in.

The third step requires that data be collected on all the variables being scrutinized in each process flow diagram. A determination is made of what could/should be happening and is compared to what is actually happening. Gaps are exposed, and plans are devised and implemented to gain the proposed improvement.

Finally, data is collected a second time. The results are compared with the initial data to determine the level of improvement that has been attained. Ongoing data collection is built into the standard operating procedures of the organization to determine the ongoing impacts of the improvements that were made.

Business-process improvement helps an organization find the simplest, fastest, and/or most cost-effective ways to do things. It may or may not involve internal and external customers but it should involve all employees. It is also possible to find ways to improve what the organization is doing by looking inside its overall industry, at best practices within and beyond that industry, and at benchmarking studies about other industries. People often are hesitant to go outside what they are most familiar with, but one can learn much about ways to improve an organization from other high-performing organizations, even from those that are in different businesses or industries.

All opportunities to improve business processes in the organization are acted on. Cost-benefit analyses are conducted before going ahead with any process improvement, whether it affects an internal customer or an external customer. Changes that don't support the attainment of business objectives are not implemented.

Measuring Process Improvement

It is very important that employees be trained in the methods of business-process improvement. Such training includes a variety of statistical and analytical tools, such as histograms and control charts; behavioral approaches, such as force-field analysis and multivoting; ways to present data, such as graphs and pie charts; and knowledge of best practices and benchmarking. It is important that every business process have a champion who "owns" the process and is committed to the improvement effort. In this case, the champion acts as a leader for the organization. This kind of leadership activity throughout the employee ranks keeps motivation levels up so that all employees become involved in making improvements.

It is important that the leader establish measurement and performance standards that can be used to improve processes. Without these, it is impossible to determine whether or not much improvement has been made. The measurements could include things such as employee focus groups, customer-satisfaction surveys, and error rates. The performance standards focus on how much, what length of time, and how many relative to the performance of a task by an individual or group of employees.

Another aspect that the leader must focus on is making sure that there are input-resource measures throughout the business-process improvement effort. Input resource measures are how leaders account for inputs that are utilized. These include personnel, technology, finances, and the physical plant. The leaders must know precisely where, when, and how every input comes into the business process. This allows them to calculate resource utilization rates. They can compare resource utilization rates from organizational function to organizational function or activity to activity to determine the most efficient practices that could be spread throughout the organization.

Regardless of the input resource and regardless of whether it produces an output for an internal customer or an external customer, the measures must be used to track all activities. This means that all inputs that are expended lead to a result for a customer. The measures are used to track all the activities associated with each input and the related result that is produced.

All departments use processes to add value. All this implies that there is some kind of reporting system that manages any variation from the business-process standards that are in place at the beginning or along the way as the process is improved.

Further Training and Reinforcement To Support Process Improvement

In addition to training all employees in how to initiate and conduct business-process improvement, leaders must make sure that when a business process is improved, everybody who needs to be trained in the new process is trained. This eliminates hesitation and conflict about what needs to be done and what doesn't need to be done. Training for employees is especially important in the area of technological solutions.

Improving business processes requires a lot of people to work together in ways they may not have worked before, so employees must learn how to work better in teams across all organizational functions. This helps to reduce conflict and increases problem-solving and decision-making abilities.

Employees must be properly rewarded for business-process improvements that they come up with. This is another aspect of the human side of the process. If employees are not rewarded individually or as part of a team, their commitment to business-process improvement will deteriorate.

The leader must also make sure that the organization has what it needs in terms of coaching skills. These may be the most neglected management and executive skills. The leader must establish a training program focused on coaching skills that help employees to find ways to execute business-process improvement projects and to encourage, manage, and reward employees involved in such projects.

Involving Customers in Process Improvement

Another consideration for the leader is being in constant touch with the organization's customers and analyzing any changing customer requirements to determine if they are consistent with what the organization holds itself responsible for. Customers also can be involved in improving business processes that directly affect them. Communication with internal and external customers should include identification of how they can provide feedback about the organization's business processes. The organization should always know if it loses a customer because of poor business processes. A database that tracks customer feedback may help to point toward processes and procedures that need to be improved.

Usually, customer service improves as a result of business-process improvements; however, what are intended as process improvements sometimes can negatively impact internal and/or external customers. Getting accurate information from customers is one way to avoid this. Such data can help the leader decide whether or not to move forward with a change in a process.

Also, it is important that customers be made aware of changed (improved) business processes so they know exactly what their role is or what they will be dealing with. One important aspect of this is making sure that customers know about internal staff changes that affect how and with whom they will conduct business with the organization.

Involving Suppliers in Process Improvement

Suppliers also need to be kept informed about business-process improvements because some processes affect the work of the suppliers. Suppliers also may be able to come up with good ideas about ways to improve business processes. To do this, suppliers need to understand the organization's supply chain. It is also a good idea to educate suppliers about the reasons for business-process improvement so that they focus on improving their own processes. If a supplier does not believe in business-process improvement, there is probably going to be some problem with that supplier in the future.

The flip side of this, of course, is that when suppliers change their business processes, they need to inform the organizations they supply. So the organization should have an agreement with each supplier that whenever one of them changes a business process that affects the other, they will notify the other.

Finally, everything that is obtained from suppliers must be monitored for quality. There is little point in improving a process within the organization if the input is flawed to begin with.

Personal Assessment of Business-Process Improvement Orientation

Questions for Reflection

1. How important is business-process improvement in your organization?

2. How do leaders hold the organization accountable for business-process improvement?

3. How much training have employees received in business-process improvement?

4. What further actions do leaders in your organization need to take to enhance its business-process improvement strategy and techniques?

5. Describe actions you would take to improve business processes in your organization.

Personal Actions

1. Description of what you did:

2. Were any resources required?

3. How were you able to sustain the effort?

4. Description of how people reacted:

5. What about the people who didn't react?

6. How creative were you?

7. Quantitative assessment of what you did: What was the impact?

8. How did you know what the impact was?

9. Ways to spread this best practice:

10. What is the possible long-term impact?

11. What's the status now? Are things still progressing?

Chapter 10

Create High-Performance Teams

W hen I was a youngster, playing team sports fascinated me because I noticed that some teams played better than others. What seemed to matter was skill, such as speed or the ability to play a particular game, as well as the ability of a group of kids to work together toward a common goal. The teams that usually won seemed to be put together with more thought about how members could contribute to the teams' goals. The teams that usually lost were put together by captains who valued only one characteristic, such as speed or size. I realized that a team's performance was no accident.

As I played more organized sports in high school, college, and as a young adult, I realized that high-performance teaming was a result of a conscious effort of a group of people to be the best they could be. Early in my career, I managed a group of nine people with quite varied skills, experience, and education. I used the understanding I had gained playing organized sports to make the team work as well as it possibly could. For the three years it was in existence, the team came in under budget and exceeded expected outcomes. A number of years later, a colleague and I worked to help a team in a large service organization to be a high-performing team. It was selected as the best team worldwide in its company, which had 68,000 employees. Still later, I received an award for high-performance teaming efforts from a group I'd consulted with. The things that I identified as necessary for high-performance teaming have since been validated by my students. High-performance teams share twelve characteristics, and it is the leader's job to provide an organizational environment in which these characteristics can grow, including 1)interactive goals, 2)resource optimization, 3)conflict management, 4)interactive leadership, 5)activity control, 6)feedback mechanisms, 7)flexibility in decision-making, 8)mutual assistance, 9)experimentation, 10)self-evaluation, 11)long-term commitment and 12)performance influence.

Characteristics of High-Performance Teams

Some tasks are meant to be done by individuals, and some are done better by teams. Once an organization decides which ones are best done by teams, it can train employees so that the characteristics of high-performance teams can be generated and applied to those specific tasks.

Interactive Goals

The first characteristic of a high-performance team is interactive goals. This means that everyone on the team makes suggestions about what the goals should be. Information about goals and objectives in an organization cascades down, and there is always some peer determination at the actual work level. High-performance teams listen to what everybody says about what his or her part of the goal attainment will entail. The discussion should be highly inclusive; everyone should have a chance to participate in developing his or her own goals as well as other people's goals and the goals of the entire team.

Another aspect of interactive goals is the belief that goals are changeable. This has two aspects. First, it means that the goals can be changed at any time in response to eternal organizational changes or external factors, such as the economy or competition. Second, it means that people's individual goals can be adjusted at any time, based on changing business requirements or task-load issues.

When people in a team are able to discuss the team's goals, when the final goals are identified, people are more apt to be committed to achieving them. They work hard toward the goals, even if they are not completely in agreement with every aspect of them, because they realize, through the discussions, that some things are simply best for the team. The feeling of being included in discussions of the goals goes a long way toward getting people committed to them.

Optimization of Resources

The second characteristic of high-performance teams is optimization of resources. Of course, everyone—whether in a business, nonprofit, government, or educational organization—believes that he or she needs more resources. High-performance teams are very successful in working with what they have. They do more with what they have and they get more out of what they have. They are successful in making their resources stretch as far as they can. One way in which they do this is by members helping one another out when work becomes backed up. Because everyone is considered part of the team's performance, even if he or she is not the principle performer on a specific task, the team members pitch in whenever needed.

Members of high-performance teams continually look for ways to help their teams use their resources more efficiently. They try different approaches. They believe in process improvement. They sort of have their own research and development effort going on. To maximize the team's performance, they never let an available resource go unused.

Conflict Management

High-performance teams are very good at conflict management. To begin with, they know that conflict is an indication that the team is growing and moving and that the members are thinking, so they welcome it. Whenever a conflict arises, whoever can contribute to solving that conflict makes himself or herself available. Rather than avoiding conflicts, the team members identify them and deal constructively with them. They know that when conflict is not attended to, it simmers and erupts, and that is not good for the team. Because of their training, they also know that there is more than one way to resolve a conflict and they know how to use conflict-resolution skills, such as being assertive, influencing, negotiating, and bargaining.

Interactive Leadership

The fourth characteristic of high-performance teams is interactive leadership. This is based on a set of common values that the team shares. One of these is the belief that leadership is based on expertise, so whoever has special expertise in the task at hand is given the responsibility to lead the rest of the team through the task. Everybody provides leadership at one time or another. Of course, there is always a formal leader in the group, based on organizational rank or some other measure, but high-performance teams rely heavily on expertise (often referred to as expert power) to guide their actions.

Activity Control

The next characteristic of high-performance teams is activity control. Each member of the team is fully aware of the end results that are sought, the team's overall task requirements, and what needs to be done. That knowledge enables the team to assign appropriate control over each activity in order that it can be accomplished most effectively. It is the activities that are "controlled," not the people.

This requires that every team member have some idea of what every other team member is doing in working on a task or project. (Unfortunately, this often is not the case in many organizations. It would be difficult for such organizations to have high-performance teams.) Members of high-performance teams see the big picture and the smaller components that make up the overall picture. In some cases, team members are capable of carrying out the tasks of other members of the team. This provides a flexibility and strength that other teams do not have.

Feedback Mechanisms

High-performance teams have feedback mechanisms. The most important aspect of this is that they consistently give praise to one another. This does not mean that they avoid constructive criticism. It merely means that they share a lot more positive feedback than most other individuals and teams in organizations normally do.

Certain skills are required to give effective feedback, both positive and constructive. High-performance team members have been trained in these skills and they practice and fine tune them so that their feedback communication is timely, specific, and accurate.

Another aspect of this is being comfortable with telling people outside the team how the team is performing. Members of high-performance teams are not interested in keeping performance secrets from others in the organization. They are proud of what they accomplish. This pride is expressed during various types of communication in ways that show how valuable the team's work is and also how others can benefit from high-performance teaming.

Flexibility in Decision Making

The seventh characteristic of high-performance teams is flexibility in decision making. The team members know that different situations require different decision-making styles. When a decision is needed, variables such as time and expertise also are considered in determining who should make it. Sometimes a couple of people in the group make the decision. Sometimes the leader of the group, based on his or her expert power, needs to make the decision. Of course, the decision maker(s) may take advantage of the organization's knowledge-management system to help them. The team members accept the fact that every situation is unique and that there are many different ways to make decisions. This is because everybody on the team has been trained in the different decision-making styles and knows how to use them appropriately. This is called behavioral flexibility and it is a very important aspect of high-performance teams. It is also another thing that makes the members of high-performance teams appreciate the fact that everybody is capable and can contribute.

Mutual Assistance

The eighth characteristic of high-performance teams is mutual assistance. It is the characteristic that separates high-performance teams from many others. When a team has mutual-assistance capability, everyone on the team is willing to help everybody else. Everyone is willing to stop doing his or her task in order to help another team member if that team member needs some help that he or she can provide. This means subjugating one's own immediate schedule or goals. Members can do this because each of them feels that he or she has "ownership" of the team's overall perform-ances and should contribute whatever is required to get the job done. The entire team's reputation depends on getting the task done, so people pitch in to help others succeed. The team members' focus is on the higher goal.

Experimentation

The ninth characteristic of high-performance teams is experimentation. This is an aspect of creativity. As we all know, children have a lot of creativity, but as people mature, various aspects of our society often function to diminish their creativity and their willingness to experiment. The result is a loss of new ideas and new ways of looking at things, which often is detrimental to the success of the organization. An important aspect of a high-performance team is that its members feel safe enough in the team to offer creative ideas and to experiment. In fact, the high-performance team nurtures creativity and encourages experimentation.

Many people fear creativity because they perceive it as lack of control. In truth, creativity has some structure. When you are using creative thinking, you are considering both the positive and negative aspects of something. High-performance team members know how to think of new possibilities and also how to evaluate those possibilities realistically. What matters is that they are flexible when considering how to get things done. They know that there is usually more than one way to do something.

Self-Evaluation

High performance teams are self-evaluating. They always know how well they are doing. Every team member is able to use a set of evaluative criteria to determine how successful the team is in terms of goal accomplishment. Every team member also knows how well he or she is doing individually. The members know whether there is a gap between their performance and what is expected of them. If there is no gap, they congratulate themselves. If there is a gap, they pitch in to eliminate the deficiency. This is where the characteristics of resource optimization, mutual assistance, and conflict management may be important.

Another aspect of self-evaluation has to do with individual actions of team members. Every team member is aware of the impact that his or her actions have on the others in the team. This is very important because what we do, what we say, and how we say it can affect others on the team. A lack of awareness would be devastating to the interactions among the team members.

The final point to be made about self-evaluation is that every team member has an opportunity to be reinforced for both individual effort and team effort. Any organizational system that has high-performing teams should pay attention to rewarding individual contributions as well as team contributions.

Long-Term Commitment

The next characteristic of high-performing teams is long-term commitment. In recent years, the workforce has become more mobile. Not as many people stay with an organization for a long period of time. The term "long-term commitment" has come to mean that a team stays together until it finishes an assigned task. This may take days, weeks, or months. In today's fluid workforce, some people will continue to contribute as part of their long-term commitment after they have left a specific team because they have special knowledge or expertise that the team needs that may not be available elsewhere in the organization. This often requires that they expend extra time and energy. The reason that long-term commitment works often is because people feel a sense of togetherness with and obligation to the members of the team. Interactive goals, interactive leadership, feedback mechanisms, and mutual assistance help to build that kind of togetherness. It is an extremely valuable aspect of high-performance teams.

Being a member of a successful team (one that has worked together well and accomplished its goal successfully) can contribute to a person's personal and professional development. If personal or professional growth is hindered by the team, it is time to reassess what the commitment should be. The success of the team and the individual should always proceed in a mutually nourishing environment. When that doesn't happen, it may be time to focus on individual contribution and/or find another team.

Performance Influence

The last characteristic of high-performance teams is performance influence. Part of performance influence is a desire to be a serious player on the team, to be willing to work hard, to cooperate, to contribute, and to perform as well as one possibly can because everyone else on the team is doing just that. This means that everybody on the team will listen to everybody else on the team because they all want to maximize performance. They want to be part of the magic of the high-performance team.

There are several other aspects of performance influence. Team members are unconcerned about status among themselves. They are not overly focused on who the formal leader is. They are not concerned with who has been on the team the longest or who is the smartest or most knowledgeable. They are concerned about the overall performance of the team. Members of high-performance teams are willing to listen if someone has an idea about how to improve individual or team performance. They respect the skills of all the other team members. They are all subject to influence by someone on the team who can help to improve overall performance. Each member is willing to make whatever changes are needed in his or her individual performance in order to make the whole team as successful as possible.

Conclusion

High-performance teams add value at every level in the organization and cross-functionally. They can function internally in the organization and with stakeholders. Leaders who invest the time and resources to create high-performance teams reap huge benefits, as the business literature consistently shows. The development of high-performance teams is an essential ingredient of organizational effectiveness, whether that organization be a business or governmental entity, a nonprofit, or an educational institution.

Robert C. Preziosi

Personal Assessment of High-Performance Teaming

Questions for Reflection

1. Describe the qualities and characteristics of the best team that you ever were a part of.

2. What about that team energized you to try to make it successful?

3. How well established is the team psychology in your organization?

4. What are some ways to build a more collaborative organization?

Personal Actions

1. Description of what you did:

2. How were you able to sustain activity?

3. Description of how people reacted:

4. What about the people who didn't react?

5. How creative were you?

6. Quantitative assessment of what you did: What was the impact?

7. How did you know what the impact was?

8. Ways to spread this best practice:

9. What is the possible long-term impact?

10. What's the payback to you?

11. What's the status now? Are things still progressing?

Chapter 11

Build a Customer-Service Management System

During a busy holiday shopping season, I selected a gift for someone, took it off the table, and walked over to two sales associates who were standing about ten feet away near a cash register. They both told me that they didn't handle that merchandise and that I needed to see a sales associate who was located thirty feet away. She wasn't there at the time, as she was on a break. I went back to the original two sales associates, and they said, "Try over there, because she is in that department, too." I went where they had directed me, and there were five people already in line. So I put the item back on the table and left the store. Something was definitely wrong with that store's customer-service management system.

It is a leader's responsibility to make sure that every aspect of the customer-service experience is positive.

Elements of Customer-Service Management

There are many things that a leader must address in establishing a customer-service management system. Remember, this is about customer-service management, not about customer service. The six critical areas that need attention are: policy, staff, training, service standards, opportunity analysis, and productivity.

Policy and Staff

Hiring

Good customer service begins with good hiring practices and good employee orientation. In hiring customer-service personnel, an organization should look for people who take pride in their work and in the organization. Job applicants should be made aware of the organization's customer-service policies when they are being interviewed. Applicants should be asked specific questions that the interviewer can use to determine if they have the appropriate service attitudes and behaviors.

Orientation

The leader must make sure that there is an orientation program that emphasizes the importance of customer service from line employees all the way up to executive management. The new-employee orientation program should explain the organization's customer-service policies and beliefs. The organization's mission, policies, and stories all should reinforce an orientation of great customer service.

The organization's culture also must include policies, procedures, and leadership styles that allow people to take pride in their work. Employees must be treated well so that they will treat the customers well. When an organization's human resource policies are viewed favorably by its employees, the employees believe that the organization cares about the people who work there. Such employees will care more about the organization's impact on its customers.

The leader needs to make sure there is a written customer-service policy statement and that all employees have seen it. They may see it during new-employee orientation; it may be posted on the machines they use to record sales; or it may be in the form of a card or job aid. The leader also has to make sure that it is people's highest priority. The policy may include the speed at which service will be delivered. It could also include: 1) how to greet a customer (whether live or electronically); 2) how to deal with unreasonable customers; and 3) the importance of a problem-solving attitude, along with steps to follow.

It is important that employees have the information they need to do their jobs when they need it. All customer-service policies and procedures should be explained in an operations manual that the leader has approved. The information in this manual may be accessed by means of a printed book, a binder, or electronically and should be given to all employees or made available to them by means of their computers. Employees should also feel free to ask colleagues or supervisors about trickier issues.

If customer-service standards are different for different parts of the business (e.g., by product, by department, by return policy), all employees should know this and it should be explained clearly in the operations manual. This is more complicated than having one policy per issue that exists throughout the organization. Similarly, there may be different service policies for different products. All employees who will be involved in customer service must be trained in how to handle these differences.

Training

Training is a critical part of customer-service management. Ongoing training sessions can address how important customer service is and emphasize that links to customer service are present regardless of what the training topic is. For customer-service personnel specifically, ongoing training should include customer-service techniques, information about new services and/or products, and information about new policies and/or procedures. It is helpful if such training includes information about competitors' products and/or services, so that employees can properly address customers' questions. The leader needs to make sure that employees receive all the training they need to perform all aspects of their jobs.

Communication is a major skill in customer service, so anyone who will be interacting with a customer should receive training in communication skills. These typically include:

- Active listening (paraphrasing for clarity)
- Types of questions
- Expressing empathy
- Staying positive

- Handling cultural differences
- Expressing oneself clearly
- Avoiding jargon
- Making reinforcing statements
- Avoiding defensiveness

Teamwork is also very important in providing customer service, so leaders should make sure that all employees receive training in teamwork. (Communication skills help with this, too.)

The training should include specific information on the organization's service goals and strategies. Strategies could be things such as response time and the cost to fix a problem, documentation requirements, and a definition of an acceptable level of satisfaction.

In addition to communication and teamwork, other typical elements of customer-service training are:

- Influencing skills
- Problem-solving skills
- Techniques for dealing with conflict
- How to calm upset customers
- Negotiation skills
- Stress-reduction techniques
- How to use technology to improve efficiency

The managers and supervisors of customer-service personnel should be trained in the same skills that are taught to their employees for improved customer-service performance. This is one of the most neglected areas in the workplace.

The organization needs to reinforce customer-service training by following up. There is a great deal in the training literature on how to reinforce training. Some useful practices are:

- Identify ways to reinforce skills learned in training
- Develop reinforcement tools
- Make reinforcement continuous
- Increase praise
- Provide meaningful rewards
- Spotlight employees who achieve
- Train supervisors to monitor performance after training
- Monitor performance often

Most importantly, training must be ongoing. There are always new training needs to be addressed.

Service Standards

Every person in the organization, from line employees to top executives, should be aware of what the organization's established customer-service standards are. Every employee needs to understand the relationship between getting things done in day-to-day operations and the organization's service standards.

Typical service standards are:

- Always be accurate
- Respond to all customer e-mails within 24 hours
- Provide the customers with options and let them choose
- Be courteous but not too friendly
- Use the customer's name
- Refer difficult customers to a supervisor
- Do not let a customer verbally abuse you
- Speak positively about the organization

When a customer-service problem arises that is beyond the skill or knowledge of an employee, the employee needs to know where to turn to ensure that it is handled properly. The line of knowledge and the line of authority must be clear to all employees.

Meetings need to be conducted frequently and regularly to inform employees of any changes in standards, practices, training, and rewards.

The leader must make sure that the organization has a way to determine if low service quality is a major factor when contracts or customers are lost. The organization also needs to have a system that reveals whether and how well the established service standards are met. This system includes data collection, analysis of the data, writing up the report, and sharing the report. It is important that every part of the organization and every individual with customer-service responsibility be aware of how well it is doing.

Encouraging and Measuring Service Improvement

Leaders need to find ways to motivate employees to promote high standards of customer service. How that is done is unique to the organization's culture and leadership approach. The bottom line is that every employee has a role in customer service that must be addressed. The leader needs to make sure that all employees are aware of how important customer service is to the success of the organization.

Almost every employee has internal customers in other departments throughout the organization. Responding to the needs of such customers based on identified standards (in the plan) helps each department or unit attain business results efficiently and effectively. Every employee must be willing to drop whatever he or she is doing in order to ensure that a customer is well served.

The customer-service system also must establish metrics for required levels of improvement (e.g., speed, courtesy, letters of praise/letters of criticism) as targets for an improved (better score) metric. The need to measure is so important. People have to know how well they are performing. The leader must spend time with his or her employees and customers discussing what to measure, how to measure and improvements needed, if necessary.

Customer-service policy should include annual plans for internal and external customers. Such plans typically include the introduction of new technology, training, staffing increases or reductions, speed of service, and new problem-solving strategies. Each plan includes metrics, so criteria are developed for each of the two different plans, for internal customers and for external customers, to measure the level of success of customer-service efforts.

The appropriate data-collection tools must be chosen. Most organizations use either a questionnaire and/or focus groups. Data are collected for external and internal customers and presented to customer-service management decision makers.

Customer-service employees should be evaluated once each quarter, rather than annually. This is accomplished through formal performance appraisal, using a standard model of performance management.

When they do well, employees must be appropriately recognized and rewarded. Such reinforcement should be part of the organization's policy, so that all employees are rewarded equitably. In particular, leaders need to make sure that employees who contribute the most to improving customer service receive appropriate rewards. All employees also must have an opportunity to discuss their jobs and get involved in issues related to their customer-service efforts.

Opportunity Analysis

Leaders use opportunity analysis when they are able to take advantage of what is going on in the organization and the customer-service arena for the betterment of the organization. They can do this by conducting surveys of internal and external customers a couple of times per year. This helps the organization to learn how the customers rate the organization's services and/or products and how well its customer service is conducted.

People who work in customer service should know the exact cost of a customer complaint or the loss of a customer. The handling of every complaint and the follow up can be documented—including who did what, how long it took, and so on. Every follow-up activity can then be evaluated in terms of cost.

Another part of opportunity analysis is the opportunity for identifying the morale in the organization. Some companies survey their employees twice per year. If morale is high, customer service is likely to be better. If morale is low, customer service is likely to be poor.

Constructive competition can be used to foster customer-service ideas and practices within an organization. Identifying "best practices" and benchmarking programs help to create constructive competition.

Because some customer-service issues flow across departments, the leader can identify which departments share certain customer issues and develop a plan for them to periodically discuss the customer-service issues they share. This can be a rich source of clarification on issues as well as suggestions for improvement in products, services, and customer service.

Productivity

The final area of customer-service management is productivity. It is important to focus on improving productivity until it can no longer be raised. It is equally important to make sure that the quality of service is maintained. A lot of procedures and processes that impact customers are done automatically by technology. Leaders must make sure that the organization's technology is working perfectly so that employees can provide the best goods and services. Similarly, any technology that speeds up and otherwise improves customer service should be purchased and used to its full capacity.

In the area of customer service, employees need to know that sacrificing long-term service for a quick fix it is not going to work. That fix is going to break down at some point. The long term must be addressed. For example, sending a service representative for the third time in two weeks does not please a customer. Replace the equipment, or the customer may be lost.

A lot of the customer-service experience is affected by cost. Leaders can expect the level of customer service that they are willing to pay for. For example, there is a cost issue in a call center, whether the average wait time is ten seconds, forty seconds, or three minutes. It depends on how many calls come in, how long the average call lasts, and to what extent the organization staffs the call center. Obviously, if the wait is too long, the organization will lose customers.

The organization needs to know how long it typically takes to resolve a customer complaint—a few minutes or a few hours or a few weeks? The customer's time is valuable, as is your staff members'. Streamline all processes that touch the customer. Speed in resolving customers' problems or issues is a major factor in customer retention.

The other side of this coin is that service quality must always override service quantity. In other words, serving exceptionally well is more important than serving a lot of people in a particular time frame. It is better in the long term to take the time to satisfy one customer than to do "quick fixes" for three customers. The dissatisfaction of the three customers will return. Productivity and service are both positively impacted when quality is the priority above quantity.

Finally, customers should know what to do if the front-line customer-service personnel do not resolve their issues. They should know that they need to call or write or e-mail only once to a manager in order to have a customer-service problem resolved. If you make it difficult for the customer to do business with you, he or she may decide to take that business elsewhere.

Personal Assessment of Customer-Service Management

Questions for Reflection

1. What do customers say about your organization?

2. How do organizational leaders communicate the importance of customer-service management?

3. Describe the system in place for monitoring organization-wide customer-service management.

4. What training programs are in place for customer service?

5. Describe your role in maintaining both internal and external customer satisfaction.

Personal Actions

1. Description of what you did:

2. Were any resources required?

3. How were you able to sustain the effort?

4. How creative were you?

5. Quantitative assessment of what you did: What was the impact?

6. How did you know what the impact was?

7. Ways to spread this best practice:

8. What is the possible long-term impact?

9. What's the payback to you?

Chapter 12

Establish a Productivity-Management System

My work experience as a teenager taught me how important efficiency is. The first job I had was delivering newspapers in the morning and afternoon. In the morning, I had to finish so that I could get to school on time; in the afternoon, I had to get back to work on the yearbook or go to basketball or baseball practice or something. I've already mentioned my job in a fast-food restaurant. Like many people, I learned from experience that speed in doing a job is important. Accuracy is also important, and speed and accuracy equal efficiency.

Most people know that the way to increase profitability is to increase efficiency and, thus, increase productivity. It is the leader's responsibility to make sure that an organization has a productivity-management system. It is through such a system that organizations, departments, and people can attain their highest levels of efficiency.

Eight Aspects of Productivity Management

There are eight important areas related to productivity in organizations (or work units or even individuals). These are: the organization's policies, leadership, objectives, resource management, performance, technology, work procedures, and staff. By bringing a set of productivity principles to bear on these areas, a leader helps the organization be as productive as it can be, given the technology available. The technology that it chooses to invest in, the quality of the employees, and the business processes it subscribes to are essential concerns.

Policies

The first requirement under policies is that the organization have a productivity mission statement that is assigned the highest priority by the leadership and that is issued to all employees. Next, managers should be required to submit productivity plans to the organization's leadership on an annual basis, so that there is an organization-wide approach to productivity. Third, there needs to be a system to monitor the results of productivity efforts—one that can be reviewed on a weekly basis. Fourth, the organization should make it a policy to involve employees in making decisions about the work they do. Fifth, all departments need to practice productivity improvement. This is not an "add on" to the work; it is essential. Sixth, the organization's power structure needs to include all necessary functions for productivity improvement. In other words, every function that impacts productivity should have a seat at the head table.

Leadership

Organizational leaders must approach productivity improvement in an action-research manner. They must be driven by the data. This can be done by conducting annual productivity audits and utilizing the information that is revealed. Knowing the state of "productivity" in an organization is a lot more than reading financial reports.

Each department and each work unit should present such a report so that the leadership of the organization has an overall picture of the level of productivity.

Organizational productivity audits normally include standards, measurements, and reporting. The productivity audit is built around a set of standards and practices that the organization believes enhance productivity. Each standard is measured using a yes/no question format. A "yes" answer means that the standard is practiced; a "no" answer means the standard is not practiced. The audit is conducted for each work unit, and each unit is accountable through the performance-management system for making the needed improvements. This occurs from line units all the way up to the executive suite.

Leaders also need to require an overall organizational productivity report annually. This report is an integrated compilation of the individual work-unit productivity reports. This allows leaders not only to assess the productivity of each work unit but also to have an overall picture of the organization's productivity. This is an example of integrative thinking—an important tool for leaders.

It is important that leaders encourage and support research-and-development efforts, not just for new products and services to deliver to customers, but also to find ways to be more productive.

Leaders should promote and implement work-improvement innovations from all levels of employees. Whether you call it business-process improvement or work-methods improvement or something else, empowering people to improve their work generates innovation and excitement. It is good for the organization to have this kind of excitement. In addition to asking employees for ideas, leaders can foster healthy competition based on the quality of those ideas rather than on the personalities of the people involved.

Leaders must emphasize teamwork; they need to ensure that collaborative efforts are the norm at all levels in the organization and across all functions. This is necessary because of the task interrelationships that exist between and among work units.

They must require a balanced effort from all work units. This means that the work loads for all work units are able to be carried out equitably with the resources the units have at their disposal. Fair and equal work loads are essential for employee motivation to become more productive.

Objectives

Productivity does not occur or improve if it is left to chance. Leaders need to provide specific and measurable productivity objectives or work with their direct reports to write these specific and measurable productivity objectives. These objectives should be aligned with the organization's vision, mission, and goals and should be sufficiently challenging yet obtainable. All employees should be fully aware of their work units' productivity objectives.

When people take actions that are part of their productivity objectives, there should be a way to identify any problems that occur in implementing those actions. There needs to be a reporting system that identifies any variation from productivity objectives. The reporting should be done on a weekly basis.

Resource Management

Resources include people, time, technology, physical space, finances, and raw materials. Everybody needs more resources, and leaders have particular responsibilities in this area. All organizational resources should be identified and accounted for in cost-center budgets. This means that each line activity and each staff activity has a separate budget so that the specifics of resource utilization are easy to track. Charge-back approaches for staff functions are not only desirable but are essential for knowing the state of productivity in the organization.

A major aspect of resource management is employee management. Leaders need to make sure that employees are spending their time in ways that contribute to task accomplishment—to the business of the organization. I read a study report that said, "Eighty-five percent of employees in organizations use the Internet to conduct personal business." How can a work unit, department, or organization be efficient

149

and productive if its employees are using company time to conduct personal business by means of the Internet? I'm assuming that "personal business" includes non-work e-mail. If that is another issue, the situation is even worse.

Every organization needs an information system that tells about its human, material, and technological resource-utilization patterns, from department to department or from level to level or from region to region. It is important to have this information because there usually are variances between those different departments, levels, or regions. The organization needs to know which places are doing better so it can use what the employees there are doing as "best practices" for the rest of the organization. There is more of a chance that more of the organization will do better when job tasks and job specifications are defined clearly and precisely. Job specifications are human resource considerations.

Another aspect of resource management is making sure that people have other types of resources available when they need them so that they can meet their schedules. If they plan poorly, that is one thing. But if they plan well and somebody else fails to get the necessary resources to them, there needs to be a review of the processes and procedures that led to the situation. In some cases, employees may control the resources that are necessary for them to meet required levels of performance. However, in many cases, someone else can influence the control of the resources in a way that makes it difficult for the employees to perform as they need to.

Likewise, the resources that serve as input must be of the quality needed to produce the quality of output that is desired. "Garbage in, garbage out" is a more serious statement than it may first appear.

Budgeting is a critical aspect of resource management. Different organizations have different approaches to budget preparation and management. Some are highly centralized, some involve employees, and some involve only managers. I believe that each work unit knows best what it needs to increase productivity and should at least be involved in discussions of its budget.

Performance

To get people to perform efficiently and productively, important performance variables must be addressed. The first is making sure that employees are completely trained in the job tasks they are expected to perform. Needed training must be made available.

The second is that the standards for work performance must be specific, measurable, and realistic and they must be communicated appropriately to employees. It also is necessary to check to make sure that employees' expectations are accurate.

There is a lot of discussion about the effects of teams in today's work environments. The primary consideration is that team-performance measures need to be identified in each work unit. This means that the tasks that need to be done by teams are identified and the tasks that need to be done by individuals are identified.

Along with this, productivity must be measured by the level of resource utilization in each work unit. It is possible that one work unit may be using more resources to get a particular result and that another work unit may be using fewer resources to get the same result. This needs to be assessed so that the efficient and inefficient practices can be identified and the information can be shared.

Technology

Technology is a major variable in productivity. Leaders must make sure that expenditures for new technology are justified by the likely improvement in productivity that will result. No one should invest in technology just because it's there; technology is just one class of resource that should be used to make the organization more productive.

Of course, leaders also need to make sure that the availability of necessary technology reflects a maximum concern for productivity. People shouldn't have to wait or stand in line to get tools that they need to do their jobs. When people have to share or wait for technological resources, they frequently slow others down. Also, technological resources must be fully functional at all times, so other resources (e.g., personnel, budgets) may need to be allocated to make this happen.

Each work unit should be totally responsible for its equipment expenditures and utilization. In many organizations these days, the IT departments establish equipment expenditures and utilization plans. Although that makes it easier to identify the expenditures for technology, it doesn't necessarily provide the best arrangement for managing and/or leading from the technology to the performance to the required output. People may not get what they need, when they need it, or how they need it.

Whoever is responsible for the purchase of technology needs to evaluate long-term considerations rather than short-term considerations. This refers to investing in technology that will provide at least three year's of usage. Technology should be viewed as an investment that enhances productivity, not as a set of toys or the single most important element in an organization's success. Investment in technology for the short term must be justified by a larger-than-normal impact on the business than is commonly seen for a certain amount of dollars invested. The goal should be to always have in place technology that is the most appropriate and that performs the way the organization needs it to perform, given the budgetary constraints. The final point is that technology that maximizes productivity must be utilized by employees at all times. If it sits around, it is a waste of money.

Work Procedures

It is imperative that the quality of the organization's products and/or services be maintained as the level of productivity increases. However, several things can hinder quality and productivity. Two of these are security and safety procedures. For example, security precautions could be unnecessarily expensive for the amount of return they provide. No one wants to undersell the need for security, but unnecessary paranoia can reduce people's productivity. On the safety side, no one would ever want to risk injury to an employee. However, it is not necessary to spend lavishly when a lower cost generates the necessary level of safety.

Time-wasting operations also can hinder productivity. A work-methods-improvement audit can help to identify slow, repetitive, or unnecessary tasks or methods. Employees can be given responsibility for identifying, and possibly changing, work methods that have an adverse effect on productivity. In a more authoritarian and centralized environment, someone else might have that responsibility, but the best scenario is for employees to have that responsibility in regard to their own work. They are the best placed to assess, for example, the relationships between people and machines and whether existing arrangements contribute to maximum productivity. They may be able to offer suggestions about the ways in which workstations are set up and so on.

Quality also can be affected by automated procedures. One cannot assume that automated equipment makes something right every time; it needs to be checked.

Organizations should conduct methods analyses on an annual basis. Methods analysis and business-process improvement are related. These productivity-improvement activities should be built into each employee's job so that, on an on going basis, individuals are looking for more efficient ways of performing their tasks. Their supervisors should always be involved in these activities.

Staff

An organization can save itself a lot of trouble by hiring people who have productivity awareness and skills. Careful interviewing can help to identify candidates that do.

At the next level, the organization must have a system by which to communicate with employees and to train them so that they are more committed to productivity improvement, are aware of productivity-improvement standards and efforts, and reflect their knowledge and commitment in their actions. Organizational e-mails, newsletters, and meetings all can be used for this purpose. Best practices inside the company should be reported so that others can use them.

The organization also needs to make sure that all employees are kept up to date in knowledge and skills. This is essential for maintaining and improving productivity.

In addition to formal employee training programs, the organization must train supervisors and managers to coach their employees for increased ability and productivity. Coaching is one of the most neglected leadership skills, but when it comes to productivity, it is very important.

Rewarding people properly for productivity improvement is extremely important. The reward system for productivity improvement has to be given a great deal of thought; it needs to be timely, accurate, and appropriate.

When a position in an organization is unfilled for some reason, it has a negative effect on productivity. Every organization must strive to retain its productive employees. When a vacancy does occur, it must put every effort into filling the position quickly.

In summary, it is the leader's responsibility to make sure that a productivity-management system is in place. Only with specific, focused attention on productivity will the organization perform as productively as it possibly can. The need for increased productivity can never be overstated.

Personal Assessment of Productivity Management

Questions for Reflection

1. What signs do you see that tell you productivity is important to your organization?

2. How would you respond to the statement "Productivity is the biggest leadership challenge of the 21st century"?

3. Other than technology, what systems are in place for maximizing productivity in your organization?

4. How would you rate the level of productivity in your own department?

5. What specific actions do leaders in your organization need to take to increase productivity?

Personal Actions

1. Description of what you did:

2. Were any resources required?

3. How were you able to sustain the effort?

4. Description of how people reacted:

5. What about the people who didn't react?

6. Quantitative assessment of what you did: What was the impact?

7. How did you know what the impact was?

8. Ways to spread this best practice:

9. What is the possible long-term impact?

10. What's the payback to you?

Chapter 13

The Values

When I was a child, I played card games, board games, athletic games, and other types of games with my friends. The games were fun and exciting because there was competition, a sense of needing to do one's best, and luck. As is normal with kids, we argued during the games as a result of different understandings of how the games were being played, the rules, and whether or not somebody was abiding by the rules.

As I look back on those games, I realize that there was a lot more going on than just play. How individuals thought about themselves and about what was important and what wasn't were strong elements. It was a matter of what you stood for. Values were expressed during the games.

These included courage, humor, honesty, optimism, trust, and fairness.

As an adult, I realized how important values are in business. Whether an individual deals with human resources, financial resources, physical resources, or technological resources, values are present in the person's decisions and actions.

Twelve Values

My research, involving over 20,000 people, and the writings of my students have revealed that twelve values are necessary for the conduct of personal and business life. They are:

1. Courage
2. Creativity
3. Diversity
4. Equity
5. Fairness
6. Honesty
7. Humor
8. Integrity
9. Optimism
10. Respect
11. Risk taking
12. Trust

Courage

Courage is the ability to make a decision and/or take necessary action when the circumstances are difficult. Often, the decision or action must be taken for the good of the group. It sometimes takes courage to make a decision or to take action based on what is right, correct, legal, or appropriate—especially if there may be negative repercussions from doing so. For example, people exhibit courage when they resist injustice or prejudice or harassment. A person may even exhibit courage when he or she sees a piece of technology that is not being used properly and brings it to the attention of someone who has the authority to correct the situation. Another example is from my own experience. A boss once told me to fire someone. I replied that I had no information about the person's performance that warranted termination. My boss said that he didn't care; he wanted the person fired. I stood up to him and told him that I wouldn't do it. I never heard any more about it from him.

Creativity

It has been said that creativity is the fuel of American business. It certainly is one of the top two or three most important fuels. Creativity is the ability to see things in different ways or to combine things in different ways or to respond in ways that no one else has imagined. Everyone has some creativity, especially during the early years of life, but societal institutions may limit its expression. In adulthood, creativity may be further repressed by the organizational culture. If an organization supports innovation and creativity, it may be re-awakened in many individuals. To support creativity, organizations must find better ways to reward and reinforce it.

Diversity

Appreciation of diversity shows itself in willingness to work with people whose characteristics (genders, ethnic roots, ages, backgrounds, beliefs, personalities, etc.), talents, and perspectives may be different. Diversity is good for business. People who appreciate diversity recognize how important it is to collect and utilize the contributions of different types of people. It is important for several reasons. First, different styles and perspectives can keep a group from making costly errors. For example, a team member who favors quick action may be complimented by one who checks the facts and possible outcomes before committing to a course of action. This kind of diversity offers a set of checks and balances. Second, diversity in ideas and approaches enriches the pool of possibilities and gives the group more on which to base decisions and plans. By taking that into account, people and organizations send the message that they believe there are a variety of options to be considered in all situations. Third, appreciation of diversity maintains harmony in the work place. Today's workers come from a wide range of backgrounds, and anyone who resists facing this reality is out of touch with contemporary life (and may be out of compliance with the law).

Equity

Equity is the quality of being fair or impartial. In practice, equity means giving everyone the same chance. Of course, there always will be some differences in workplace opportunities because of requirements regarding skills, knowledge, seniority, and so on and because people decide to include or not to include themselves. But equity should be available as far as possible. For example, if an examination is to be given in order to determine who is qualified for a particular position, anyone who may possibly be qualified and who wishes to take the examination should be able to do so. Practicing equity goes a long way in displaying the organization's belief that all people have equal rights and fundamental worth.

Fairness

Something that is fair is free from bias, dishonesty, or injustice. Fairness also refers to playing by the rules of the game. When the situation is fair, everyone who decides to "play the game" is afforded the same advantages and considerations by those who are judging, refereeing, or managing. The rules and regulations are always the main drivers in fairness. They are meant to put all players at the same starting position and to inform them of what is required or allowed and what is not.

Being fair also involves being willing to join an activity or project that will respect everyone's abilities and efforts.

Honesty

Honesty is telling the truth. The truth is important because people make decisions or take actions based on the information they are given by others. Honesty also is being straightforward, open, and verifiable. It can be very tempting to not be honest in order to save face or to avoid being the bearer of bad news. However, honesty, because its impact can be so wide, is truly "the best policy" in all business activity.

Humor

There are several uses of humor in organizations. Humor is used by effective communicators so that others understand the points that are being made while experiencing some fun at the same time. People are more likely to remember the points because the humor has made them more memorable. Humor also can help to build relationships among people. Because laughter is an effective way to release tension, humor can be used to provide a lighter side or a moment of respite in a tense situation. People and organizations are more healthy when they laugh. Because of all the important impacts it has, humor is an important value to an organization. Of course, it is important to remember that respect for all is an important element of the expression of humor.

Integrity

Integrity is uncompromising adherence to moral principles or ethics. We speak of "a person of integrity" to describe someone who consistently displays honesty and trustworthiness. This is the type of person that others respect. We all know people that have integrity and we all know people who seem to lack it. The caution is not to accept situational ethics in determining a course of action. Situational ethics suggests that every situation is different and the "right" action is determined based on all the variables in the situation. The problem with situational ethics is that it can be used to justify almost any action.

Optimism

I learned optimism from my grandfather. He was always positive and upbeat. He worked very hard as a head chef in restaurants in New York and Miami Beach. Being a head chef is hard work, and it is difficult to remain optimistic in an environment with that kind of pressure. Whenever I met any of his business associates, they were quick to point out that working with my grandfather was a wonderful experience because he always saw the bright side of things.

We now know that optimistic people create more energy in organizations. The reverse is also probably true: people who are pessimistic drain the energy. Moreover, it is common knowledge that optimistic leaders are the best leaders. One can be optimistic and still be realistic. It is one's mindset that determines whether one sees the glass as half empty or half full. Optimistic people can see reasonable expectations of successful outcomes.

In contrast, pessimistic people expect trouble and failure. It has been said that all negative emotions, including anger, stem from fear of some kind of loss. In general, pessimists have negative expectations for one of three reasons: 1) because they are *afraid* (e.g., of being disappointed or embarrassed or wrong), so they expect little in order to protect themselves; 2) because they have experienced such (traumatic) negative results in the past that they are *conditioned* to expect them in the future; or 3) because they are *angry* about something and transfer their anger into negativity. Whatever the reason for it, a pessimistic outlook takes its toll on the person expressing such views and on all those who must interact with him or her. In terms of teamwork or leadership, it certainly is not motivating!

Realistic optimism, on the other hand, is motivating and energizing.

Respect

Treating others with respect is very important in personal and business relationships. It allows for appropriate interpersonal conduct. Showing respect is contagious. When you treat someone well, he or she is more apt to treat you well in return. In addition, people want to do business with those that treat them and others with respect.

Showing a lack of respect for others (in front of them or not in front of them) also is contagious. It has negative effects on the viewers or hearers as well as on the persons in question.

Respect is recognition of others because of their qualities. These qualities may be basic human worth, personal traits (e.g., honesty), roles in life, abilities, experience, education, or expertise. Respect based on a person's experience, education, or role in life is not the same as elitism, which is based on preconceived exclusion of people who do or do not belong to certain groups.

Risk Taking

Risk taking is engaging in behavior that is deemed necessary or right, despite the uncertainty of the outcome. Everyone takes some necessary risks in life; even a turtle has to stick its head out once in a while in order to function in its environment. Those who value risk taking believe that, without it, many good opportunities are passed up.

Risk taking should always be based on evaluation of the probability of success if one were to take (or not take) a particular action or try a new approach. Often, after collecting and studying the data pertinent to a particular course of action, one may determine that it isn't such a big risk after all. The point is that although risk taking often can lead to success, it is very important to make sure that there is a reasonably good probability of success before you invest human, financial, physical, and/or technological resources.

Trust

Trust has to do with credibility and reliability. I trust you when I feel that I have reason to believe what you tell me. I trust you when I have experienced you delivering what you said you would deliver. It has been said that trust is the most essential element in building a high-performance team or organization. The power of trust in personal and business life is awesome. This is partly true because trust is based on the existence of other things we value, such as honesty, integrity, reliability, consistency, fairness, and courage. Without trust there can be no solid interpersonal relationships. Trust also is important in teamwork. When there is trust, people know that they can rely on one another—that someone will speak up for them or cover their backs because it is the right thing to do.

Conclusion

The twelve values discussed above have surfaced continually over the past twenty years in my experiences with entrepreneurs, executives, educators, consultants, and other professionals. Of course, other values have been identified as being important in a work environment. However, these twelve have been identified as being most important to success in personal and business life.

You will note that the values are related to one another and interact with one another. For example, trust and respect grow out of evidence of honesty, integrity, fairness, and so on. Learning to appreciate diversity increases respect for a wider range of people. Risk taking requires courage. Successful risk taking generates optimism.

It should be obvious that these values must be aligned in one's personal and professional lives; it is pretty well impossible to hold values personally and exclude them from one's professional life, and it is difficult to demonstrate values in your professional life if you do not espouse them personally. Personal situations and business situations may require different behaviors, and in certain situations one value may be emphasized over another. Nevertheless, one's behaviors always emanate from one's values.

High-performance organizations hold values that some other organizations do not subscribe to. It is important for an organization's leaders to think about what its core values are and to identify them for the organizational members. It is even more important for the leaders to exemplify these values in all their personal and business interactions.

The organization's values must drive the decisions and actions that individuals within the organization take. The twelve tasks that are a leader's main responsibilities are carried out within the context of the identified organizational values.

Over time, one or more organizational values (e.g., risk taking, equity) may change. Leaders need to stay aware of which of the organization's values should be emphasized at any particular point in time in the evolution of the organization.

Personal Assessment of Values

Questions for Reflection

1. What are your organization's values?

2. What actions are taken when it becomes very clear that an employee's values are not consistent with the organization's values?

3. How consistent are your personal values with the organization's values?

4. What actions do you take to increase your values consistency?

Personal Actions

1. Description of what you did:

2. How were you able to sustain the effort?

3. Description of how people reacted:

4. Quantitative assessment of what you did: What was the impact?

5. How did you know what the impact was?

6. Ways to spread this best practice:

7. What is the possible long-term impact?

8. What's the payback to you?

Chapter 14

The Zone Capstone

I decided some time ago that commitment plays the key role in leadership success. Leaders and followers must be committed to one another and to the organization. This way of thinking causes people to enable, enlist, empower, engage, and energize one another. I also now think that the leader needs to commit to a variety of leadership actions. This is more than committing to an idea. It is doing. It is behavior. It is leadership action.

This book is about leadership action. It identifies the key tasks for leaders and gives advice about leadership behaviors and the values that ought to drive them. It includes frameworks and suggestions. Theory has consciously been avoided. The only things that remain to be offered are some perspectives. This chapter focuses on perspectives that leaders would be wise to consider.

Perspectives on Leadership

1. The total leader focuses on more than tasks and values. Well-trained line employees, supervisors, managers, and executives are best examples of the technical side of the business, but lead-

ers must never forget the people side. Combining the people side of the business with the technical produces a harmonious whole. An organization's results can be maximized by joining together its technical skills and its people skills.

2. Perhaps the most important element in an organization is productivity. This book discusses the key tasks and attitudes that impact productivity more than any other book on leadership. This is especially important in our times; after decades of being the #1 country in terms of competitiveness, the United States has fallen to #6!

3. It is probably obvious by now that a leader's approach typically emerges out of his or her own experience. With that as a starting point, one's leadership attitudes and behaviors need to be filtered through a framework. *The Leadership Road* provides such a framework. It is an effective framework because it comes from where the action is: leadership behavior in organizations.

4. It is important to remember that the each of the elements of this book is a part of the total package. For example, values only mean something when they are translated into behaviors. An important message of this book is that success is measured not only in the bottom line but also in whether what is accomplished and how is it accomplished is consistent with what the organization and its people believe in.

5. Inherent in leadership growth and development is the need for self-knowledge. A leader must develop the skills of observing, recalling, and assessing leadership situations that he or she has

engaged in. Self-awareness and reflection are essential if a leader is to improve his or her leadership behaviors.

6. As a person moves from one level of leadership success to the next, he or she will realize that leadership development is a never-ending journey. This is true because the people and the situations that require leadership action will continue to change. Task priorities will change. Personal and organizational values may even change. Leaders need to change, too; adaptability is one of the most important human skills and is even more important in ever-evolving leadership situations. Each set of leader actions will tend to be unique because of these situational changes. Therefore, every leader will need to pay attention to the differences in people and situations and discover his or her own set of evolving best practices. To do this, it is wise to keep track of high-impact leadership experiences. A leader may keep an electronic file for reference and review—one that easily can be updated. An example of such a file is found in the Appendix, "Leadership Best Practices Worksheet." It can be used for the collection and storage of behavioral options for personal use.

Someone once asked me if I would like to fill a leadership void in an organization that I had already provided leadership for. It had been a very successful experience and left the organization in a state of positive accomplishment, but there was difficulty in getting someone to take the organization to the next level. I said I'd be happy to, but was curious about the issue of not being able to find someone else. I had always felt that no one was indispensable. I wasn't either as I found out. I was told, though, that my legacy was humility. I had served the organization without riding on a white horse. At that point, I made a lifelong commitment to leading so that others could have the spotlight shining on them.

Appendix

Leadership Best-Practices Worksheet

1. Aspect of leadership that I applied:

a)   What task was I working on?

b)   What value(s) was(were) in play?

2. Description of what I did:

3. Description of how people reacted:

4. Description of what was accomplished:

---

5. Quantitative assessment of what I did:

6. Strategy for personal application in the future:

7. Ways to spread this best practice to other leaders:

About the Author

Robert C. Preziosi was named "Faculty Member of the Year in 2003." He is a professor of management with the Wayne Huizenga School of Business and Entrepreneurship at Nova Southeastern University. He designed the curriculum for the Master's Degree in Leadership and is Faculty Chair for HRM. He was the recipient of the school's first Excellence in Teaching Award. In December 2000 he was named Professor of the Decade. He has been vice president of management development and training for a Fortune 50 company. In 1984, he was given the Outstanding Contribution to HRD Award by the American Society for Training and Development. In 1990, he received the Torch Award, the highest leadership award that the society can give. He was named HRD Professional of the Year for 1991. He has been named to the first edition of *International Who's Who in Quality*. In June 1996, he received his second Torch Award from the society-the first time ASTD has given a second Torch Award to one individual.

Bob has worked as a human resource director, line manager, business school dean, and leadership training administrator. He has been responsible for leadership training and education in every one of his professional positions. He has been published in various national publications, including *Quality Review*. He has been a consultant to consultants, educator of educators, and a trainer of trainers.

Bob's management education consulting experience includes all levels of management with many organizations including American Express, AT&T, FP&L, NCCI, and Pollo Tropical and a large number of hospitals, banks, and government organizations at the local, state and federal levels. He has trained entire departments of trainers. He has been interviewed for *Fortune*, *Meeting Management*, *Savings Institutions*, *Technical and Skills Training*, the *Miami Herald*, and the *Sun-Sentinel*. Recently, *Training and Development* referred to him as a member of Who's Who in HRD. In 2007 his autobiography appeared in a book of the 50 quintessential Adult Educators in North America for the 21st century.

He as a B.A. degree in social science and an M.Ed. degree in educational psychology. He received his doctoral degree in management. He has a special certification in coaching skills, participative leadership, and consulting skills, and has completed study at Harvard University's Institute for the Management of Lifelong Education. He is listed in *Who's Who in Finance and Industry*, *Who's Who in the World*, and *Who's Who in American Education*. Four times he has been selected for *Who's Who Among America's Teachers*.

Bob has been a national seminar leader for the American Management Association and Dun & Bradstreet. He has presented to regional, national, and international conferences on various aspects of leadership, management, and adult learning. He has recorded a video titled "The High Performing Trainer," and a six-part audio program titled, "Executive Success Strategies," in addition to his six-part audio series on "Maximizing Adult Learning". He was the Editor of the Pfeiffer Annual on HRM. Currently he is the editor of the Pfeiffer Annual on Management Development.

LaVergne, TN USA
02 March 2011
218580LV00002B/20/P